Stephanie was about to head back to shore in the canoe, when she heard a motorboat coming closer. She glanced over her shoulder. The boat roared past her, leaving behind a gigantic wake. The wave lifted the canoe—and before Stephanie could react, the canoe had tipped over and dumped her into the water.

"Help—" Stephanie started to scream.

She plunged into the cold lake water face first. The jolt of the sudden fall—and the shock of the cold water—made her gasp.

Whoever is driving that motorboat is a royal jerk, she thought as she came to the surface. Her vision was blurry as she coughed out the water she had inhaled.

Stephanie rubbed the water from her eyes and focused on the figure swimming toward her. *That must be one of the jerks from the boat*, she thought angrily. As the swimmer came slowly closer, she could tell it was a boy.

"Hey!" the boy called. He had nearly reached her. "Are you okay?" he asked again. He stopped swimming, treading water nearby.

Stephanie opened her mouth to yell at him—and gasped.

She stared at the boy's face and nearly swallowed another mouthful of water.

He was absolutely gorgeous!

FULL HOUSE™: Stephanie novels

Available from MINSTREL Books

FULL HOUSE™ C L U B
Stephanie

Truth or Dare

**Based on the hit Warner Bros.
TV series**

Kathy Clark

A Parachute Press Book

A
MINSTREL®
BOOK

Published by POCKET BOOKS
New York   London   Toronto   Sydney   Singapore

A MINSTREL PAPERBACK *Original*

A Minstrel Book published by
POCKET BOOKS, a division of Simon & Schuster Inc.
1230 Avenue of the Americas, New York, NY 10020

A PARACHUTE PRESS BOOK

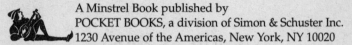

Copyright © and ™ 2000 by Warner Bros.

ISBN: 0-671-04126-6

First Minstrel Books printing June 2000

10 9 8 7 6 5 4 3 2 1

Cover photo by Schultz Photography

Printed in the U.S.A.

CHAPTER
1

◆ ◂ ▪ ◆

"What have you got in this trunk, Darcy?" Stephanie Tanner complained. "A dead body?" Her long blond hair fell into her eyes as she dragged one end of the heavy black metal trunk up the steps to the camp lodge. Her best friend, Darcy Powell, pushed the other end.

"Hey, I brought only what was on the list!" Darcy reached the top step and gently set down her end of the trunk.

"Oh, sure. I know you—you brought *three* of everything on the list," Stephanie said with a laugh. It was Sunday afternoon, and they had just arrived at Camp Sail-Away.

Darcy straightened up and smoothed the

1

creases out of her khaki cargo shorts. She wore a bright orange shirt that looked great against her dark brown skin. "How long were we on that bus, anyway?" she asked, curling a strand of her black hair behind her ear.

Allie Taylor mounted the steps. "It seemed like forever." She dropped a big green duffel bag at her feet and shook out her legs. "I thought my legs would fall off from sitting still for so long. And if I have to listen to one more verse of 'Ninety-nine Bottles of Pop,' I'll scream. I really will." She grabbed her brush from her purse to neaten her short, wavy brown hair.

"Come on, Darcy," Stephanie said. "It's your turn to help me carry *my* trunk." She bounded down to the bottom of the steps and started dragging her trunk up.

Anna Rice stretched her arms over her head and gazed out at the summer camp property from the porch of the lodge. "I'm so glad we're here!" she said. Her silver bracelets slid down one freckled arm. She was wearing a sundress she had stitched together, patchwork style, from different fabrics. "This place is beautiful. Woods, trees, that fresh mountain air . . ."

"You sound like a TV commercial for an air

freshener," Darcy teased her. "Where's your bag?"

"Right here," Anna replied, patting the knapsack that hung from her shoulder. "I brought only the bare minimum. I figured I'd pick up some stuff while I'm here—paint some new T-shirts, buy a camp sweatshirt, you know."

Kayla Norris wheeled her suitcase up the ramp to the porch. "I brought everything on the list and then some." Kayla was tall and thin, with long blond hair like Stephanie's. She usually wore it in a braid with ribbons tied at the end. "I hate being unprepared."

"Speaking of lists, I can't wait to see the list of CITs," Stephanie said. She and Darcy shoved her trunk against the wall of the porch. "I hope I made it off the waiting list. Maybe someone decided to stay home and baby-sit instead of coming to camp." Deep down, Stephanie knew that wasn't likely. Who would choose baby-sitting over camp? Especially if you were a counselor-in-training.

Stephanie had waited until the last minute to send in her Camp Sail-Away application—and she had been too late to catch one of the CIT positions her friends all had. Still, she was glad to be at camp for the next few weeks—even though she'd miss her family back home in San Francisco.

"Let's go inside and find out," Anna suggested.

Stephanie and her friends walked into the lodge, which was the camp's dining room and events center. It was a large rectangular building constructed from timber logs. The group headed for the table marked "Registration."

"Is this where we eat all our meals?" Kayla peered around at the tables. Old black and white photographs covered the walls, showing how the camp had developed over the years.

"Eat the meals—and serve them," Allie reminded her. "And clean up afterward."

"Being a CIT sounds *so* glamorous," Darcy joked as she pretended to flip her hair. "You're going to miss so much, Steph."

"Welcome to Camp Sail-Away!" One of the counselors warmly greeted Stephanie and her friends as they approached the table. Other counselors at the table were busy checking in other campers. "I'm Julia. Who are *you* all?" Julia had a southern accent and long, curly brown hair. She wore a white polo shirt with "Camp Sail-Away" written in green over the pocket.

"I'm Darcy." Darcy held her hand out to shake

Julia's. "This is Anna, Kayla, Allie, and Stephanie. We're all going to be CITs!" she said excitedly.

Stephanie cleared her throat. "Except me. Unless, of course, there has been a cancellation?"

Julia shook her head. "Not that I've heard of yet."

Stephanie felt her heart sink. She wouldn't get to be a CIT for the summer. That meant she wouldn't be able to spend nearly as much time with her friends as she wanted. And she wouldn't be responsible for the younger campers or teaching a sport. "Isn't there anything I can do?" she asked.

Julia shook her head. "Sorry. All the CITs checked in already—you guys are the last ones." She glanced down at a list on her clipboard. "But guess what?" she added. "You're in my cabin, Stephanie. I'll make sure you have a great time. And don't worry about not being a CIT—there's always next summer."

Julia finished checking them in and gave them their informational packets. She told them about their first meeting and gave them all maps of the camp.

"Come on, Stephanie—cheer up!" Anna said as they left the table. "You get to take the summer off."

"You can laugh at us while we run around after a bunch of six-year-olds," Kayla added.

"Let's go find our cabins," Allie said. "We can unpack and get settled."

Stephanie glanced at her watch. "I don't think we have time. Our first all-camp meeting is in five minutes!"

"You guys are welcome to leave your bags here. We have a little golf cart we use to drop campers' bags at their cabins," Julia offered. "You can take a look around the camp."

"Sounds great," Stephanie said. "Thanks!"

"Let's take a quick tour," Anna suggested. "I want to see the arts and crafts shed—"

"The horse stables," Allie said.

"The tennis court," Darcy said.

"The lake!" both Kayla and Stephanie cried at once.

Stephanie laughed as she studied the map. "I think that's a little too far, actually. How about if we visit the horses?"

They headed down a grassy path to the stables. They had just arrived at the edge of a fenced pasture, when they heard a loud bell ringing.

"We don't want to be late for the first meeting!" Allie said. "We'd better run!"

6

Stephanie took a deep breath of woodsy air. "You know what?" she commented as they made their way back toward the lodge. "Even if I don't get to be a CIT, I think this summer's going to be great."

"Yeah," Allie giggled. "Especially with a boys' camp just across there!" She pointed to the woods.

"I wasn't talking about *that*." Stephanie swatted Allie on the arm with her long shoelace key chain.

"Well, I was," Allie replied. "I think it'll be totally fun having a brother camp so close by."

"So do I," Darcy said.

Anna stepped over a short tree stump in the path. "How many girls are at this camp, anyway?"

"About a hundred," Darcy told her. "Why?"

"Because I see them outside the lodge—and it looks like they all got here before us."

The girls scrambled ahead to the grassy clearing in front of the lodge. Stephanie looked around for a place to sit.

Several counselors in Camp Sail-Away T-shirts were seated on the lodge's wide front steps. On the top step, a man and a woman stood behind a podium, talking to each other.

Stephanie perched on a rock at the back of the crowd and looked up at the lodge porch.

The man behind the podium turned to the group and spoke into a microphone. "Welcome to Camp Sail-Away. I'm Kenneth McCready, your camp director. And this is Heather O'Donnell, the assistant director."

A short woman with shoulder-length black hair stepped forward. She and Mr. McCready wore the same uniform—a green polo shirt and khaki shorts. But Heather wore her polo shirt buttoned all the way to the top. "I'm Heather O'Donnell, assistant camp director here at Camp Sail-Away," she announced.

"Didn't Mr. McCready just say that?" Stephanie whispered to Darcy.

"Greetings, campers," Heather continued in a stiff, formal voice. "Welcome to camp. Please make sure you read all the rules and regulations in your welcome packet—and follow them to the letter."

"Oh, *she* sounds like fun," Darcy whispered to Stephanie.

Mr. McCready nodded. "Thank you, er, Heather. So—does anyone here know the Sail-Away

cheer?" he asked. "All you returning campers—
please show the new campers how it's done!"

The counselors stood up, as did several
campers. Heather blew a whistle and everyone
started yelling the camp cheer. Heather marched
around the porch in time to the chant. She
reminded Stephanie of an army sergeant.

Stephanie noticed a very loud group sitting
way up front. She stared at the five girls, who all
wore pink T-shirts and pink hair ribbons. *It can't
be*, Stephanie thought. Her disbelief grew as she
watched the girls. *No—it's impossible.*

"Allie?" Stephanie asked. "Are those girls who
I think they are?"

Allie followed Stephanie's gaze and gasped.
"Oh, no!" she cried. "It's the Flamingoes!"

CHAPTER
2

"So, what do we do?" Darcy asked when the meeting broke up about fifteen minutes later.

"We go say hello—I guess." Stephanie had just barely gotten over the shock of seeing the Flamingoes—five girls she knew from home in San Francisco.

"Can you believe it?" Kayla asked. "I mean, what are the chances?"

"Really small," Stephanie said. "Suddenly I'm feeling incredibly unlucky."

All through the meeting, Stephanie had struggled with the idea of sharing another summer vacation with the Flamingoes. It seemed like no matter what she did, the Flamingoes were there.

Years ago they had asked Stephanie to join their exclusive club—and she turned them down. Ever since then, they'd had an intense rivalry with Stephanie and her friends.

"Well, we're stuck with them," Stephanie said. "Maybe we could actually all get along this summer."

"Stephanie!" her friends protested at once.

"We've tried that before," Darcy pointed out. "It never works."

Stephanie shrugged. "Maybe not. But we don't have much of a choice, do we?"

"You're probably right," Allie admitted. "I'll go talk to Jenny—at least we have horseback riding in common. Do you want to come with me?"

"Why not?" Stephanie said. As she walked beside Allie, she noticed the Flamingoes were all standing in a circle around Mr. McCready, talking and laughing.

What did they do to make such a good impression? she wondered. *Camp started only an hour ago, and already they're best buddies with the director!*

When they reached the group, Allie cheerfully called out, "Jenny, hi! How are you?"

Jenny Lyons turned to Allie. "Oh, hi," she said in a bored voice. She wore pink sneakers and

11

short pink shorts and a white camp T-shirt. A pink clip held her wavy brown hair back from her face.

"Hi, everyone." Stephanie waved to the entire group. "It's pretty funny, seeing you guys here."

"What's funny about it?" Darah Judson put her hands on her hips and glared at Stephanie. Darah wore a black miniskirt, a hot-pink baby T, and chunky black sandals. Her long hair was curled up into a bun with a pink pencil stuck through it. *She isn't exactly dressed for summer camp,* Stephanie thought.

"Oh, nothing. It's just a pretty wild coincidence—that's all," Stephanie said.

"Yes. It certainly is." Darah frowned. "Just wild. In fact, I was just asking Rene—how did we get so *lucky?*"

"I was wondering the same thing," Stephanie shot back. The summer had just started, and already she was being insulted by the Flamingoes. So much for getting along! She stared at Rene Salter, who was wearing a bubble-gum-colored tank top and tan cargo shorts.

"So, Jenny, have you gone to see the stables yet?" Allie asked. "Have you checked out the horses?"

12

Jenny smiled and nodded. "Actually, I've been down there a couple of times."

"Already? Wow," Allie commented. "I tried, but we didn't get here soon enough. You really are a dedicated rider, huh?"

"I try to be," Jenny said smugly. "So, are you planning on taking riding as one of your activities?"

"Actually, I was planning to help teach it," Allie said confidently. "I'm a CIT, so—"

"Me, too," Jenny said excitedly. "And I know *I* get to work down at the stables—that's already been settled. I don't know if any *other* CITs can work there, though." She spun around and tapped Mr. McCready on the arm. "Dad? How many horses do we have?"

Stephanie's jaw dropped. "Did you hear what I just heard?" she whispered to Allie.

"The camp director is her *dad?*" Allie's forehead creased.

Rene Salter smiled. "He's her stepfather," she told Stephanie.

"And we've known him for a really long time," Rene added. "He thinks of us as his *own* daughters."

"You know, Jenny, I'm not sure how many horses we have," Mr. McCready began.

"Sixteen!" Heather, the assistant director, chimed in. "However, a few of them are foals and not ready for riding yet."

"Thanks, Heather," Jenny said with a smile. She turned back to Allie. "So there might be something you could help with. I don't know about being a riding *instructor,* though."

Stephanie couldn't stand Jenny's superior attitude toward Allie. Jenny knew that Allie was fantastic with horses and an excellent rider—just like her. So why did she have to act like she was better than Allie? Just because her stepfather ran the camp?

Mr. McCready stepped closer to Jenny. "Who are your new friends, Jenny?"

New friends? More like old enemies, Stephanie thought.

"We go way back, actually," Jenny said. "This is Allie."

"Allie! You're one of our CITs," Mr. McCready said warmly. "Welcome, welcome. It's great to have you here."

"Yeah. Really great." Rene rolled her eyes. "I can't get over the excitement." She and Darah whispered to each other and laughed.

Stephanie cleared her throat. She wasn't going

to let the Flamingoes get to her. "Hi, Mr. McCready. I'm Stephanie Tanner. Could I talk to you about being a CIT?"

"You mean—you're not a CIT, Stephanie? How absolutely *tragic*," Rene commented.

Darah and Tiffany Schroder giggled.

I should have known Rene would say something obnoxious like that, Stephanie thought. She had had more unpleasant experiences with Rene than she cared to remember: like the time Rene stole her boyfriend, the time Rene tried to steal her summer job. . . . The list went on and on.

"Ah, Stephanie. I remember your application," Mr. McCready said. "At least I think I do—there were quite a few."

"I remember it," Heather said. "Stephanie's was the one that arrived *late*."

"Sorry about that," Stephanie said. "But I mailed it before the deadline—"

"That doesn't count," Heather said briskly.

"Sorry," Stephanie said. "Anyway, I know you have enough CITs, but I was wondering if there's any way you could make an exception. Are there any openings at all? In any of the activities?"

"An . . . an exception?" Heather sputtered. "But that would be breaking our late-application rule.

15

And, anyway, we can't have too many CITs. That would throw off all the numbers!"

"Let's check those numbers. Now, hold on, where did I put my list . . ." Mr. McCready started searching his short pockets.

"I have it right here, sir." Heather quickly handed him a clipboard with three different high-lighters attached to it by strings. "I've color-coded everything for you."

"Um, thank you, Heather. And please don't call me sir," Mr. McCready said.

"Oh. Well. Okay—Mr. M., then." Heather pointed to a place on the pink sheet of paper. "There's the CIT list right there, and, as you can see, we're full."

He scanned it quickly. "Heather's right. All the CITs Camp Sail-Away needs are standing right here: Darah, Rene, Cynthia, Jenny . . ."

All the Flamingoes are CITs—and I'm not? Oh, no! Stephanie thought. *They'll never let me forget this!*

"And of course there's Darcy, Anna, Kayla, Allie, and Suzanne," Mr. McCready finished the list. "Sorry, Stephanie. But I'm positive you'll have a great summer anyway."

"Next summer apply on time," Heather said.

16

"You have to follow the rules just like everyone else!"

Stephanie gave a short nod. "Right. Of course." She wondered how much time she'd have to spend with Heather over the summer. She hoped it wasn't much!

"Stephanie, you look really disappointed. And I know *exactly* how you feel," Tiffany said. She straightened a pink rhinestone barrette that held her long blond bangs to one side.

"You do?" Somehow, Stephanie doubted that very much.

"*I'm* the only one among my friends who isn't a CIT this summer, too," Tiffany complained. She popped her gum.

"Oh, well, um . . . did you apply, too?" Stephanie asked.

Tiffany nodded. "But for some reason, they didn't take me. And I really, really wanted to be a CIT." She looked up at Mr. McCready with sad blue eyes, then turned to Stephanie. "They get tons of privileges," she said under her breath. "Not to mention a free camp T-shirt *and* a camp duffel bag."

Stephanie smiled uneasily. She wasn't sure how she felt about being allies with Tiffany. She'd never had anything in common with a Flamingo—and she didn't plan on starting now!

Stephanie opened the door of the log cabin and stepped inside. This was where she'd be living for the next few weeks. It looked cozy, clean, and warm, with built-in bunk beds along the walls. Stephanie spotted Julia sitting at a table in the middle of the room.

"Hi—Stephanie, right?" Julia asked. Stephanie nodded. "We've assigned you to that bunk over there—" Julia pointed to a top bunk near the window. "Right above Leah Hollings. Does that sound okay?"

"Sounds great!" Stephanie said. She headed to the bunk, where a girl was sitting with her back to Stephanie. "Leah?" Stephanie asked.

The girl stood up and turned around. Stephanie's heart sank.

"Welcome to the Brown Bear cabin, Stephanie," Rene Salter said. She gave a wide grin. "I'm your CIT!"

CHAPTER
3

Stephanie stared at Rene in shock. "You? My CIT?"

"That's right!" Rene chirped. "And we're going to have *lots* of fun together—aren't we, Stephanie?" She flashed Stephanie a big fake smile. "Aren't we?"

"Oh, yeah," Stephanie mumbled. "We're going to have tons of fun together."

I didn't think we'd have a CIT! she thought in annoyance. *This cabin's for the older girls. We're old enough to take care of ourselves.*

Her dismay grew as the news sank in. *Rene will find some way to use this against me,* Stephanie realized. *She'll try to ruin my whole summer.*

"Rene is here only temporarily," the head counselor, Julia, said. "After the training period, all the CITs will be reassigned. But maybe we'll get lucky and she'll be back here with us!"

Stephanie crossed her fingers behind her back. *Or maybe we'll get lucky and Rene will be reassigned*, she thought. *To Siberia!*

"So, who wants to head over to the lake?" Stephanie stretched her arms over her head on Monday morning. She'd already been to her first meeting, had had breakfast at the lodge, and had completed her morning cabin chores. She was wearing her swimsuit under a pair of soccer shorts and a T-shirt. She couldn't wait to get into the water.

"I'm ready." Stephanie's bunkmate, Leah Hollings, threw her towel around her neck. "I signed up for swimming. But it's so early—the water's going to be cold. All I really want to do is lie on the dock in the sun and do nothing."

Stephanie laughed. "We get a rest period this afternoon, don't we? Can you make it until then?"

Jasmine James pulled her bathing suit out of a trunk at the foot of her bed. "Let me change really quickly and I'll go with you guys."

"Cool!" Stephanie searched on her bedside table for her sunglasses. She really liked her cabinmates, Leah and Jasmine. They'd stayed up late the night before, talking and getting to know one another. Then Rene had told them they were keeping everyone else awake. It didn't matter that the rest of the cabin had stayed up talking, too.

Rene stood in the doorway to block their exit. "Stephanie, you can't go anywhere," she said.

"What?" Stephanie asked.

"First, you have to check out the chore wheel for today," Rene said.

"I did," Stephanie said. "We did our chores—remember?"

"Then how come I just found this on the floor?" Rene held up her index finger. Dirt covered the tip.

Stephanie couldn't believe it. Rene had to be the only CIT in camp who was using a white-glove test on the cabin floor. "I swept it," Stephanie said. "I swear."

"Maybe you did, but you'll have to do it again." Rene leaned down and picked up a pine needle. "See this?"

Stephanie turned to Leah and Jasmine. "You guys can go ahead—this might take a while."

"No, we'll wait for you. I don't know why we need a CIT anyway," Leah grumbled to Stephanie. "She's our age. She doesn't know any more than we do."

"And she's acting like such a know-it-all," Jasmine added.

Stephanie smiled to herself as she plucked pine needles out of the crack between floorboards. Her cabinmates had known Rene for only a few hours, but they already had the same opinion of her as Stephanie did.

Stephanie finished sweeping the floor and turned to Rene. "Can I go now?"

Rene walked around the cabin slowly. She looked under each bunk bed. She ran her hand along the baseboard.

Stephanie sighed. "I kind of need to get to the lake *today*."

Behind her she could hear Leah and Jasmine giggling.

Rene stood up and faced Stephanie. "You did an okay job, so I guess you can go now. But don't be so sloppy next time."

Yes, sir! Stephanie thought. Rene was acting like an army sergeant. *Heather must have trained her.* "All right. Thanks." Stephanie grabbed her towel and rushed out the door.

"What is with her?" Jasmine asked. "She's taking her job a little too seriously."

Stephanie shrugged. Her new friends didn't need to know her entire history with Rene—it would only make things worse. She and Rene were going to have to get along better this summer or she'd never last.

"Oh, my gosh." Jasmine stopped as the lake came into view. Sun sparkled on the water and small waves lapped against the shore. "What a gorgeous day!"

"What a gorgeous *lake,*" Stephanie said.

"No wonder it's called Camp Sail-Away." Leah stopped at the lake's edge and took a deep breath. She tilted her face to the sun. "I think I'll get on a sailboat and stay on it all day!"

"Come on—let's check out the boathouse," Stephanie said.

"You go ahead. I want to stay right here." Jasmine slipped off her sandals and waded into the lake. "Wow, it's colder than I thought it would be. Put your feet in, Leah."

Stephanie left her new friends behind and headed to the boathouse. Counselors were carrying boats out of the long wooden building and setting them on the sandy beach: canoes, sailboats, even kayaks and Windsurfers. *Whether I'm a CIT or not, this is the place I want to be*, Stephanie thought.

She walked into the boathouse and nearly bumped into another girl. "Oops—sorry!" Stephanie apologized. She noticed the name tag on the girl's shirt: SUZANNE MULLIGAN, CIT.

"No problem," Suzanne said. "I'm Suzanne."

"I'm Stephanie."

"Hey, I saw you yesterday with all the other CITs. Are you on waterfront duty, too?" Suzanne asked eagerly.

Stephanie shook her head. "Actually, I'm not a CIT. I wanted to be, but I applied too late. All the spots were taken."

"That's rotten," Suzanne said. "Well, I have to find the other waterfront CITs. See you around, Stephanie."

Stephanie stood by the entrance to the boathouse as Terri, the head counselor from Allie's cabin, carried a stack of yellow and orange life jackets past her. "Anything I can do to help?" Stephanie asked.

"Well, let me see." Terri set the stack down on the dock. Her short platinum hair reflected the bright morning sun. "You're Stephanie, right? Allie's friend from home?"

Stephanie nodded.

"Allie told me you were hoping to be a CIT, too," Terri said. "Sorry—it's a very popular job."

"I guess so," Stephanie said. She glanced at all the counselors and CITs milling around. She saw Rene, Darah, Kayla, and Suzanne waiting together in a group for instructions. *I wish I were with them*, she thought as she waved to Kayla.

"Allie also told me you're the best sailor in the bunch," Terri went on. "Tell me some of the things you've done on the water so I can keep you in mind for next year."

"Well, I spent one summer running a sort of mini-camp at a pool for little kids," Stephanie said. "With my friends, of course. And then we worked for one summer at a sailing club. And last summer, we did an adventure program where we did white-water rafting, hiking, and windsurfing."

"Pretty impressive!" Terri remarked. "Hey, since you're so experienced on the water, could you do me a favor?"

"Sure," Stephanie said. "What is it?"

"Well, last week we spent some time fixing things around camp and patching up boats. I put a big patch on this canoe, but I need to make sure it's seaworthy. Could you take it out for a test run while I go over some things with the new CITs?"

"Sure, I'd be glad to," Stephanie replied. She slipped a life jacket around her shoulders and tightened the straps. Terri handed her a paddle, and together they carried the green fiberglass canoe to the water. The Camp Sail-Away logo was painted in white on the bow of the boat.

"Just paddle out around the raft and come right back, okay?" Terri said. "Your sailing class starts in a few minutes. I'll be watching you, so wave if you have any trouble."

"No problem!" Stephanie sat in the rear of the canoe. Terri gave her a shove and Stephanie started paddling. She kept her eyes peeled for any rocks underneath the surface. She had to make sure she didn't bump into any rocks and spring a new leak in the canoe. *Good thing there's not much wind this morning*, Stephanie thought as she neared the large square raft. Paddling a canoe alone wasn't easy—and if it was windy, it would be impossible. Stephanie checked out the raft. She could picture herself lying on it after a long swim. She saw another beach and docks directly across the lake, about a half-mile or so away. That was the boys' camp, Clearwater.

I wonder when we'll get to meet them, Stephanie thought. She glanced up as she heard a motorboat coming down the lake. Someone was waterskiing. She watched the skier jump over a swell and land smoothly. Whoever it was, he or she was very good.

Stephanie rounded the raft and was about to head back to shore, when she heard the motorboat coming closer. She glanced over her shoulder. The boat roared past her, leaving behind a gigantic wake. The wave lifted the canoe—and before Stephanie could react, the canoe had tipped over and dumped her into the water.

"Help—" Stephanie started to scream.

She plunged into the cold lake water facefirst. The shock of the sudden fall—and the jolt of the cold water—made her gasp.

Whoever is driving that motorboat is a royal jerk, she thought as she came to the surface. Her vision was blurry as she coughed out the water she had inhaled.

"Are you okay?" a boy's voice called to her.

Stephanie rubbed the water from her eyes and focused on the figure swimming toward her. *That must be one of the jerks from the boat,* she thought angrily. As the swimmer came slowly closer, she could tell it was a boy.

He's probably from the boys' camp, Stephanie thought. *When he gets here, I'll let him know what I think of him! He can't just zoom around the lake like that, knocking over people in canoes!*

"Hey!" the boy called. He had nearly reached her. "Are you okay?" he asked again. He stopped swimming, treading water nearby.

Stephanie opened her mouth to yell at him— and gasped.

She stared at the boy's face and nearly swallowed another mouthful of water.

He was absolutely gorgeous!

CHAPTER 4

♦ ◄ ♦ ♦

The boy grinned at Stephanie as she stared at him, spitting out a mouthful of water.

"Hey—don't drink up the whole lake," the boy teased. "Save some water for the rest of us."

Say something funny. Say something funny, Stephanie told herself. But she couldn't say a single word. Her eyes were glued to the boy in front of her.

He was a very good swimmer, with strong, tanned shoulders and mischievous green eyes. He wore a silver chain around his neck that glistened in the sun. Though his hair was wet and plastered to his head, Stephanie could tell it was quite blond from the sun.

She quickly dunked her head into the lake to smooth back her hair. When she resurfaced, the boy was still staring at her. Their eyes met for a second, and then Stephanie glanced away.

"You're not hurt, are you?" the boy asked.

Stephanie shook her head. "I'm fine."

"Well, good. But you'd better grab your canoe before it floats away."

"What? Oh, yeah." *I must look like an idiot*, she thought as she swam over to the capsized canoe and reached for it. *Pull yourself together, Steph!*

"My name's Luke. Luke Hayes." The boy pushed the other end of the canoe toward Stephanie. "I'm sorry we made you capsize. We shouldn't have brought the boat so close to you."

"Were you waterskiing?" Stephanie asked.

Luke paddled over to grab a ski that was floating on the lake. "Yeah. That was me."

"You're really good," Stephanie said. Then she felt stupid. Of course he knew he was good. And here she was, looking like a drowned rat.

"Thanks," Luke said. "Anyway, are you sure you're all right? Whoever you are?"

"I'm Stephanie Tanner. And I'm sure I'm all right."

Luke gazed at her, and she felt a little shiver of excitement. Or was it the cold water? "Yeah," he said. "You look all right."

Stephanie blushed. To cover her embarrassment, she tugged on the canoe to right it.

"Let me help," Luke offered. He reached for the canoe and ended up grabbing Stephanie's arm instead.

Stephanie felt her face flame red as she looked down at his hand on her arm.

"Oops. Sorry." Luke let her go.

"Oh, uh, it's okay," Stephanie said. She rocked the canoe upright, then quickly hauled herself inside. *Thank goodness I did that right,* she thought with relief. Righting a canoe was tricky, and Stephanie knew she could have easily embarrassed herself by messing it up.

"Nice job," Luke told her. "I guess I'm not the only one who spends a lot of time on the water." He handed Stephanie her paddle, which was floating beside him.

Stephanie smiled. "No, I guess not."

"So, you're spending the summer at Sail-Away?" Luke asked.

"How did you know?" Stephanie asked.

"One, you're about a hundred yards from camp

31

property, and two, you're *in* camp property."
Luke pointed to the camp logo on the canoe.

Stephanie felt her face turn pink again. "Right.
And I assume *you're* going to Clearwater?"

"Brilliant deduction," Luke replied, still treading water. "We ought to be detectives. Tanner and
Hayes, Private Eyes. Whenever a canoe paddle
goes missing, whenever a cookie is stolen from
the dining hall, whenever a junior camper skins
his knee—we'll be there." He made a mock-
serious face and saluted.

Stephanie laughed. She was so busy gazing into
Luke's green eyes that she barely noticed the
motorboat pulling up a few yards away. When
the driver cut the motor, it sputtered loudly as it
died. Stephanie snapped back to reality as she
looked over at the two boys in the boat.

"Charlie! What took you so long?" Luke called.
He turned to Stephanie. "Charlie's a counselor at
Clearwater—the other guy is Max. He's a CIT."

"Hi, Charlie. Hi, Max!" Stephanie waved to
both of them. Charlie looked about twenty-two.
Max was Stephanie's age, with blue eyes and
curly brown hair. He's cute, too, Stephanie
thought. But not nearly so cute as Luke.

"What happened?" Charlie asked.

"The wake swamped her canoe," Luke replied. "I stopped to make sure she was okay." He heaved himself over the side of the motorboat and stood up.

Wow. He looks even better out of the water than he did in it, Stephanie thought, gazing at his tanned body. She forced herself to look back at Charlie.

"Oh, no! I'm sorry," Charlie called out. "I didn't see you."

"It's really my fault," Luke admitted. "I'm always yelling at Charlie to go faster."

"And then you can't hang on when he does," Max teased him.

"Like you can," Luke shot back.

Charlie shrugged apologetically at Stephanie. "Every summer, Max and Luke try to out-ski and out-climb each other," Charlie explained. "Somehow they've talked me into taking them out in the boat extra early so they can practice even more. I've never seen such an intense rivalry."

I have. Stephanie thought of her competitions with the Flamingoes.

Suddenly there was a loud whistle coming from shore. Stephanie turned around and saw Rene on the dock. Rene waved to her, then blew the whistle again. "Stephanie!" she called through cupped hands.

"Looks like you're wanted over at Sail-Away," Charlie said.

"I should get going," Stephanie said. "My sailing class is starting. Nice meeting you guys!" She flashed a little smile at Luke. Then she steered the canoe toward shore and started paddling as swiftly as she could.

Wow, she thought as she cruised toward the beach. *It's only my second day at camp, and I've already met the cutest boy I've ever seen!* She glanced across the shore toward the boys' boathouse and beach. *I wonder when I'll be lucky enough to run into Luke again*, she thought.

"Stephanie, what were you *doing* out there?" Rene demanded as soon as Stephanie stepped out of the canoe in shallow water.

"I was testing this canoe—for Terri," Stephanie said. She looked around for the counselor.

"Whose permission did you have?" Rene asked.

"Uh . . . *Terri's?*" Stephanie said.

"Well, Terri's not in charge of the waterfront," Rene said.

And you are? Stephanie wanted to say.

"Stephanie!" Terri appeared from inside the boathouse. "I saw what happened out there. Did the canoe hold up okay? Did *you?*"

"I'm fine," Stephanie said. "And the canoe seemed okay, but it's kind of hard to tell now." She pointed to the water in the bottom of the boat. "Does anyone have a bucket? I need to start bailing."

"You should be able to find a sponge or two around. I have to run—I see someone trying to raise a sail!" Terri hurried off toward a group of beginning sailors.

Rene frowned at Stephanie. "You know, you're ten minutes late for your intermediate class. You held up everyone else."

"I'm sorry," Stephanie said as she located a large sponge on top of another canoe. "It was that motorboat's fault—"

"It's not their fault you took that boat out," Rene said. "Without permission."

"I just told you!" Stephanie said. "Terri said—"

"Terri's not your counselor," Rene said. "Look. I'm your supervising CIT. And if you really want to help down here, you should bail out all the boats. Clean out the cobwebs. Air the life preservers. That sort of thing."

"You know, you can't tell me what to do." Stephanie squeezed water out of the sponge. She felt like throwing it at Rene.

"Actually"—Rene pointed to the "CAMP SAIL-AWAY CIT on her T-shirt—"I *can*."

"Not down here at the waterfront," Stephanie shot back. "Now if you'll excuse me, I have to finish bailing this boat." She dipped the sponge into the water at the bottom of the canoe.

"You better shape up," Rene said. "You've got a long summer ahead of you—as a *camper!*"

Stephanie glared at Rene's back as she walked away. Rene was really letting this CIT thing go to her head. Stephanie was already sick of it, and this was only Day One!

CHAPTER
5

♦ ◂ ◆ ♦

"Darcy!" Stephanie rushed across the tennis court to greet her friend. She hoped Darcy was going to teach her tennis class. After the morning she'd had with Rene, she was ready for a little fun.

Darcy bounced a green ball on her tennis racket. "Hi, Steph. How's it going?" She was wearing a baseball cap, a white T-shirt, and a short blue tennis skirt.

"Where were you at lunch?" Stephanie asked. She took a tube of lip balm out of her pocket and rubbed it across her lips.

"All the CITs had lunch with Heather and Mr. McCready," Darcy explained.

"Oh." Stephanie couldn't help feeling left out.

"It was totally fun, except that *you* weren't there." Darcy poked Stephanie with her racket. "You know, I asked Heather why there couldn't be just one more CIT. She gave me a lecture about the exact numbers they needed and how they have this perfect proportion of campers to counselors. And so on and so on."

Stephanie laughed. "Well, thanks for trying."

"No problem. I'll *keep* trying," Darcy promised.

Campers began to gather around the edge of the tennis courts, waiting for their classes to start. Stephanie took a racket from the basket sitting on the court. "Want to volley a little?"

"I can't—I've got to teach the little kids," Darcy said. "The real beginners. Another CIT is supposed to take your class. . . ." Darcy's forehead creased. She suddenly looked upset. "Here she comes now."

"Who?" Stephanie turned around.

Cynthia Hanson was marching toward them, two tennis rackets in a bag slung around her shoulder. She wore a pink tennis dress. With Cynthia was a younger girl, about ten, who was also wearing pink. The girl looked almost exactly like Cynthia.

"Okay if we take this court?" Cynthia dropped

her bag onto the court and took out the tennis rackets. "This is my little sister, Marguerite. We'll play over here."

"But, Cynthia," Darcy said. "You're supposed to teach the intermediate players."

"I *am* intermediate," Marguerite said. "I've taken lessons since I was six."

"Oh. Well, okay," Darcy said. "But, uh . . . you're going to coach the other campers, too. Right?" she asked Cynthia.

"Of course. After I warm up." Cynthia picked up a giant wire bucket of tennis balls. She and Marguerite took opposite sides of the court. "You guys wait there. I'll be only ten or fifteen minutes!" Cynthia called to Stephanie and the waiting campers.

Ten or fifteen minutes? That's almost a quarter of the class time! Stephanie thought. She took a seat on the ground and watched Cynthia and Marguerite hit the ball to each other. More campers filtered down to the courts and took seats around her. Meanwhile, Darcy was teaching drills to the beginning players. All of them were playing, while Stephanie's group sat and waited for Cynthia and Marguerite to stop warming up.

"I thought this was a class," a girl sitting next to Stephanie commented.

"I know," another girl added. "Not an exhibition."

"We've been waiting ten minutes—in another half hour, the activity will be over," the first girl complained.

"I think I'll say something." Stephanie got to her feet and loudly cleared her throat. "Um, guys? I know you're in the middle of warming up. But we'd kind of like to play, too."

Cynthia missed a shot from Marguerite as she turned to listen to Stephanie. "What did you say?"

"Well, we're all just sitting here. And it might be nice if we could play," Stephanie suggested.

"You want to play?" Cynthia smiled, a devilish look in her eye. "Okay. How about if I hit a bunch of balls to each of you guys and evaluate your skill level? I can see what you need help with."

"Sounds great," Stephanie said.

"Good. Why don't you collect all the balls into that wire basket, Stephanie—while I get to know the other girls?" Cynthia asked.

I can't believe I'm being ordered around by two Flamingoes now! Stephanie frowned but went ahead with the task. She picked up a few dozen tennis balls while Cynthia and Marguerite stood around and sipped water from sports bottles.

Then all the girls formed a line on the opposite side of the court from Cynthia.

"Stephanie, since you were so nice to pick up all the tennis balls, you can go first," Cynthia called over the net.

Stephanie adjusted her grip and bounced on the toes of her sneakers. She wanted to be ready for Cynthia's first shot. Stephanie hadn't played tennis in a few months, but she was usually pretty good.

Cynthia hit a hard serve to her. Stephanie saw the ball coming toward her and swung. The strings on her racket made a loud *whoosh*ing sound. She had completely missed the ball!

Marguerite laughed. Stephanie turned to frown at her just as Cynthia hit another serve to her. This one hit the court and bounced off Stephanie's arm! Behind her, Stephanie heard giggles from the other campers.

"Um, Stephanie? There *is* a beginner's class right over there." Cynthia pointed with her racket at Darcy's court.

"I'll get better," Stephanie said as she moved to the back of the line.

"You'll have to," Cynthia said. "Because you can't get much worse."

Stephanie glared at Cynthia, who was grinning. *Cynthia's not a CIT*, Stephanie thought. *She's a JIT—Jerk In Training. Only she doesn't need much practice—she's already a pro!*

"So how was *your* first day of camp?" Allie moved over on the wooden bench so Stephanie could sit beside her in the dining room.

Stephanie groaned. "Terrible." She grabbed a dinner roll from the basket on the table and took a bite.

"Really?" Allie asked. "Why?"

"*You* try having the Flamingoes as your CITs," Stephanie said as she tore the roll into pieces. "They're doing everything they can to make my summer rotten."

"Well, that figures," Allie said. "But maybe tomorrow will be better."

"I don't see how," Stephanie complained. "With Rene as my cabin CIT? She's on my back all the time."

"That's only a temporary assignment, though," Allie reminded her. "After our training period, we all get reassigned."

"True," Stephanie mused. "But how long, exactly, is this training period?"

"Steph, I know you're upset because you're not a CIT," Allie said. "But you're still going to have a great summer."

"Easy for you to say. *You* don't have Rene ordering you around. *You* don't have Cynthia flinging tennis balls at your head," Stephanie grumbled.

Allie giggled, then put her hand over her mouth. "Sorry. It's just that . . . that sounds funny."

Stephanie smiled despite herself. She really had made a fool of herself on the tennis court. At least she'd provided a few laughs for everyone.

"Anyway, what about that cute guy you met? You can't leave without finding out more about him," Allie argued.

"True." Stephanie thought about Luke for a minute. She still couldn't get the image of his waterskiing out of her head. Not to mention his incredibly gorgeous face. He made being on the water look so natural and effortless. Stephanie couldn't picture herself ever looking—or feeling—that comfortable on a pair of waterskis.

"So, anyway, Allie," Stephanie asked, "how do you like being a CIT?"

"It's not easy," Allie said. "But it's fun. The girls in my cabin are all nine years old. They go everywhere together. They're inseparable."

"Like we used to be?" Stephanie grinned.

"Exactly! But they won't separate for *anything*— not even for their activities," Allie said. "We had to convince them that they all couldn't ride the same horse at the same time."

Stephanie laughed. Then she gazed around the dining room. "I see Darcy and Anna . . . where's Kayla? Do you guys all eat with your cabins?"

Allie nodded. "I'm waiting for mine now. If one's late, they're *all* late. And we're all about to miss dinner."

"So are you, Stephanie," a voice behind her said. "You'll be in big trouble if you don't get moving."

Stephanie sighed as she turned around. She'd know that voice anywhere. "What's the big deal, Rene?" she asked.

"Everyone in the Brown Bear cabin eats dinner together," Rene said. "That's one of the rules, remember? So you can't sit here." She frowned at Allie. "Where's your cabin, anyway?"

"They're *coming*," Allie said. "Not that it's any of your business."

"What's the matter? Can't you get them to follow their schedules?" Rene asked in a snotty voice.

Stephanie pushed her chair back and stood up. "Listen, Rene, you have no right to talk to Allie that way." She was about to say more, when there was a commotion in the open doorway.

A circle of campers had formed around someone, and people were asking, "Are you okay?" and "What happened?"

Stephanie, Allie, and Rene all rushed toward the door. Stephanie gasped as she saw Suzanne, one of the waterfront CITs, being helped into the dining room by Heather and Mr. McCready. Suzanne's right leg was in a cast that went from her foot to her thigh.

"Poor Suzanne!" Stephanie said to Allie.

"That looks like a bad break," Allie noted.

"Give us some room, people!" Heather called. She and Mr. McCready guided Suzanne to a chair and carefully lowered her into it.

"We took her into town to see the doctor. Suzanne has a serious fracture," Heather announced. "Now, don't forget, Suzanne—elevate your foot."

Stephanie crouched by Suzanne's chair. "I'm so

sorry you're hurt. That must have been really painful!"

Suzanne nodded.

"How did it happen?" Darcy asked.

"This is really stupid, so I might as well tell everyone at once and get it over with," Suzanne said, her face turning pink. "I was down at the lake, when I realized I left my whistle in my cabin. I was running late, so I took a shortcut through the woods. My foot went into this hole and my ankle twisted and then my leg completely snapped. I feel so stupid," Suzanne said.

"Don't," Darcy told her. "That stuff happens."

"Yeah, but on the first day of camp? Now I won't be able to be a CIT this summer. I definitely can't help with anything athletic," Suzanne said sadly.

"I know," Anna cried. "You could help me teach arts and crafts. I had so many kids in class today, I could hardly remember everyone's names—not to mention keep track of all the supplies."

Suzanne's face brightened. "I love to draw," she said. "What do you say?" she asked Mr. McCready. "Can I work in arts and crafts?"

"Certainly!" Mr. McCready scratched his head.

"But we'll have to get someone to replace you down at the lake."

"I'll get *right* on it, Mr. M.," Heather promised. She pulled a notepad out of her shorts pocket. A pen was clipped to her baseball cap.

Stephanie cleared her throat and stepped toward Mr. McCready. "I could replace Suzanne," she offered. "I have tons of experience in sailing and swimming—and all kinds of water sports. I'll do a great job if you give me a chance."

Mr. McCready turned to Heather. "What do you think?"

"I don't know. That would be quite unusual. Completely against camp tradition," Heather said.

"Well, we have to do *something*," Mr. McCready said.

While they put their heads together to discuss it, Stephanie glanced over her shoulder to see what the scuffling noise was behind her. Rene and Cynthia had their hands on Tiffany's shoulders and were pushing her forward through the crowd.

"Mr. McCready?" Tiffany asked as Rene gave her a final push forward. She tripped and stubbed her toe on a chair. She was wearing sandals. "Ow!"

"What's wrong?" Mr. McCready gave her a concerned look.

"Don't tell me you broke your leg, too," Heather said.

"No, it's just—" Tiffany winced as she rubbed her foot. "*I* want the CIT job, too."

CHAPTER
6

◆ ◀ ◣ ◆

"You do?" Heather asked.

"You *do?*" Stephanie added. Then she remembered Tiffany telling her how she had applied for the job, too. They'd both been rejected the first time around. But Stephanie had been rejected because her application was late. Who knew why they turned down Tiffany? Stephanie was sure there'd been a good reason.

"Yes, I do," Tiffany said strongly. "I've always wanted to be a CIT. Always. Since I was a little girl."

Darcy and Allie looked at Stephanie with raised eyebrows. Stephanie shrugged.

"And I have—um—a lot of experience," Tiffany went on.

Heather smiled at her. "Okay. Tell us about it."

Tiffany looked stunned. "Tell you . . . ?"

"Tiffany, you know what she means," Rene urged. "Tell her how you've been a baby-sitter for years. And how you're a great swimmer and sailor. You even went rafting and hiking last summer, and—"

"Oh, yeah, I forgot I did all that," Tiffany said.

"Tiffany was sort of the leader of our group," Darah went on. "She's so capable, she helps us through everything."

"Really." Mr. McCready nodded. He looked impressed.

Stephanie felt like she was going to be sick. Nothing could be further from the truth. Tiffany could barely keep her head above water. She thought a sailboat boom was an explosion. And she hardly knew which end of the paddle to put in the water.

"I'm really qualified for the job, too," Stephanie said. "Remember my application? The only reason I didn't get a CIT position the first time was that my application was late."

"Well . . . being on time is important when you're a CIT," Darah said.

"That's right. Isn't it, Dad?" Jenny asked. "And Tiffany is *known* for being prompt."

Tiffany smiled uneasily.

Allie stepped forward into the crowd surrounding Heather and Mr. McCready. "Stephanie's an excellent swimmer and sailor. She taught me how to do half the stuff I know how to do. She even won an award last summer for being a good sport."

"Is that true, Stephanie?" Heather asked.

Stephanie felt herself start to blush. "Yes. And I love being down at the lake. I know how to windsurf and canoe—"

"Could have fooled me," Rene muttered under her breath. "She capsized today."

Stephanie hoped Mr. McCready hadn't heard her. "I promise I won't let you down."

"And I promise I'll be a perfect CIT!" Tiffany exclaimed.

"Give us a few minutes, would you?" Mr. McCready asked. "Heather and I need to discuss this and decide what to do here."

"Yes, this is *quite* unusual." Heather looked baffled. "My numbers . . . they're going to be all off if we have two CITs doing each job from now on."

"You could just give *me* the job," Tiffany suggested.

"No, that wouldn't be fair," Heather said.

"You know what might work?" Mr. McCready said. "They could draw straws. That would be extremely fair."

"But it wouldn't take into account their skills," Heather said. "I have another idea, if I could borrow your ear for a moment. Let's go into the kitchen and talk in private."

She and Mr. McCready left the dining room. Stephanie's friends gathered in a tight circle around her. The Flamingoes hovered around Tiffany.

"Did you *hear* all that?" Anna shook her head. "They must have been talking about some other Tiffany."

"Maybe she'd make a good CIT," Kayla said with a shrug.

"What?" Allie cried.

"Sure. If one of the activities was applying nail polish." Kayla giggled.

"I don't mind Tiffany that much. But I bet she doesn't even know what the initials *CIT* stand for," Darcy said.

"What do you think they're going to decide?" Stephanie asked.

"I have no idea," Anna said. "I mean, if this was logical, they'd choose you. But they do have to be fair about it."

The swinging doors to the kitchen opened. Heather and Mr. McCready walked out and approached Stephanie and Tiffany.

"Girls? We've made our decision," Mr. McCready said. "Actually, it was Heather's brilliant idea."

Heather beamed at him. "Thanks, Mr. M. Okay, guys. You ready for the exciting news?"

"Yes!" Stephanie kept her fingers crossed behind her back. *Please let me be the next CIT*, she thought.

"We're going to have a contest," Heather said. "The CIT contest will consist of two parts. The first part will focus on your cabin skills. The second part will concentrate on your outdoor skills, especially down at the waterfront, where you'll need to help out."

Sounds great, Stephanie thought. *I know I can beat Tiffany in any contest!*

"Now, I don't have it all worked out yet. So we'll have the competition starting Wednesday— that will give me all of Tuesday to plan it," Heather explained. "I hope that's enough time. Of course, I could stay up all night and work out a schedule, too."

She makes it sound so serious, Stephanie thought. *What exactly is she planning?*

"Anyway, may the best CIT win!" Heather threw a fist into the air.

Stephanie turned to Darcy. "Well, that doesn't sound bad."

"Not at all," Darcy said. "You'll definitely win—although Heather sounds like she's a little too into this."

"She lives for organization," Anna told the group. "She came by the arts and crafts shed today and made me label everything. She even alphabetized the paint colors."

Allie put her hand on Stephanie's shoulder. "You have nothing to worry about. If Heather is that hyper about being organized and on top of everything, she'll see right away that Tiffany's nothing like that."

They started moving back toward their tables. Stephanie and Kayla found themselves walking behind a few of the Flamingoes.

"I'll never win," Tiffany was saying to Rene. "I don't have a chance. I might as well quit now."

"Tiffany! Come on, you have to do it," Rene said. "I want to keep being Stephanie's CIT. It's way too much fun to give up that job."

Stephanie and Kayla glanced at each other. "Lucky you," Kayla whispered.

"And if you win, you get to be a CIT like the rest of us. We have to stick together. Flamingoes forever . . . right, Tiffany?" Rene asked.

"But Stephanie's so good at everything," Tiffany whined. "I can't beat her in a contest."

"Yes, you can," Rene said. "And you will—don't worry. We'll all help you beat Stephanie!"

I don't like the sound of that, Stephanie thought. *When Rene and the rest of the Flamingoes really want something—look out!*

CHAPTER
7

♦ ◄ ◗ ♦

"I'm so excited!" Allie said early Tuesday evening. Stephanie and her friends were heading down the path toward Camp Clearwater. All of the older girls had been invited to watch a movie at the boys' lodge. "We're going to see real live boys! I hope they're cute."

It was about a twenty-minute walk through the woods around the lake. Luckily, the sun hadn't set yet, so the girls could see where they were going.

"I thought we'd never get to meet them," Darcy added as she carefully stepped over a small patch of wildflowers.

"You guys! We haven't even been at camp a

whole *week* yet," Stephanie said. She swung her hair out of her face. She hoped she looked okay. She was wearing denim overall shorts over a striped T-shirt.

"So? Who wants to wait all summer?" Allie skipped along the path.

A few minutes later they passed through a gate that led to the camp. Stephanie heard shouting ahead of them in the woods. Soon they came upon a group of guys gathered around the boys' obstacle course. Stephanie recognized the two guys from the motorboat the day before—Max, the CIT with curly brown hair, and Charlie, the counselor.

Their obstacle course looks even harder than ours, Stephanie thought as she checked it out. The climbing wall was a few feet higher than the one at Sail-Away, and there were rope bridges, climbing ropes, hurdles, and a wobbly-looking log to balance on. Overhead was a series of tightropes strung between platforms at different heights. The lowest rope was close enough for Stephanie to reach, but the highest loomed above her, about as high as a two-story building.

Then she spotted Luke, surrounded by a few guys she didn't know.

"I'll bet you one week of cabin chores," Luke was saying to Max. "If you lose, you have to do my chores for a week."

"It's a bet." Max shook Luke's hand. Luke turned and started toward a ladder that led up to a platform.

"Luke, don't do it," Charlie ordered. Luke just grinned at him.

"What are they talking about?" Stephanie asked Charlie. "What is Luke going to do?"

"Something very stupid," Charlie replied. "Max bet him he couldn't walk that tightrope up there."

Stephanie stared up at the highest tightrope. *Hey,* she realized with a shock. *There's no net! If he falls, he could really hurt himself!*

Luke climbed the ladder toward the top platform. He hesitated for a second, then gingerly stepped out onto the rope.

"That's Luke—the guy I met on the lake," Stephanie whispered to her friends.

"He's going to walk that thing?" Darcy asked. "Is he crazy?"

"He's not crazy," Stephanie insisted, though she wasn't so sure. Her heart pounded as she watched Luke take another few steps. "He's daring."

"Luke!" Charlie called. "Come down from there! Don't be stupid."

"Who's being stupid?" Luke shouted. "This is fun!" He took another careful step. He'd managed to walk almost halfway across the rope.

"That's fun?" Allie said. "I could never do that—not even three feet off the ground!"

"Me either," Kayla agreed. "I couldn't even walk a straight line on a piece of rope *on* the ground."

Stephanie watched as Luke took three quick steps in succession. *Wow*, she thought. *He's really talented.*

"Luke! Come on, we're not fooling around," Charlie, the counselor, shouted. "The movie's about to start. If you don't get down now, I'll come up there and get you."

"Well, since you put it *that* way." Luke turned on his toes and walked quickly back to the platform. Then he climbed down the steps until he reached the lowest platform. He grabbed the rope there and swung to the ground, nearly landing right at Stephanie's feet!

"Whoa! Look out, Tarzan!" Darcy joked.

"Hi, Stephanie," Luke said. "What's up?"

"Um . . . you?" Stephanie joked. Luke laughed. "Everyone? Meet Luke Hayes," she said.

"Do you always make such grand entrances?" Anna asked.

"Only when there's a crowd," Luke said as he tossed the rope back up to the platform. "Did I mention I used to be with the circus?"

"Yeah—he was the bearded lady," Max joked.

"That wasn't me," Luke retorted. "That was your mother!"

Max barked out a quick laugh and punched Luke lightly on the arm. The two boys ran off toward the lodge, pushing and shoving each other.

"He sure knows how to catch people's attention," Allie said to Stephanie as they followed Max, Luke, and the other boys up the hill. "And he's even better-looking than you said."

"Maybe," Kayla said. "But he's also reckless. That rope must be at least two stories high. He could have killed himself!"

"If they didn't want anyone to walk across that rope, why did they put it there?" Stephanie countered.

"Steph has a point," Darcy agreed.

"Besides, I don't think he's reckless. He's . . . adventurous," Stephanie said. *And totally, completely cute!*

*　　*　　*

Stephanie and Darcy were having a cup of juice after the movie, when Luke and a tall boy with dark brown hair and cool glasses walked up to them.

"So, did you like the movie?" Luke asked Stephanie.

"That depends. Which one?" Stephanie asked.

The night had started out with a hilarious camp bloopers video, followed by a corny old western. The campers had roared with laughter at the bloopers video, which showed counselors making complete fools of themselves. One counselor belly flopped into the lake, another crashed his sailboat into the docks, and a third tripped in the dining hall and fell facefirst into his dinner.

"I have a feeling that video was not an official part of tonight's program," Darcy said with a laugh.

"Sure it was," Luke said. "The counselors just didn't know it was coming, that's all." He laughed and shook his head.

Stephanie folded her arms across her chest and raised an eyebrow. "Why do I get the feeling *you* had something to do with it?" she asked.

"I'm not saying I did . . . and I'm not saying I

didn't." Luke smiled at her. "And I'm not saying Keith here did . . . and I'm not saying he didn't."

"Ah-ha! So it's a conspiracy," Darcy said. She turned to the tall boy with brown hair. "Hi, I'm Darcy."

"Hi," Keith said. "This is Luke—"

"We met him already," Darcy said. "He was swinging from a vine, I think. Beating on his chest, yelling—that sort of thing."

"That's Luke." Keith smiled. "We try to keep him chained to his bunk, but he keeps escaping."

Darcy and Stephanie cracked up laughing.

"So, Darcy—care to join me for a cookie?" Keith offered. He pointed toward a table full of refreshments on the other side of the room. "The camp cook makes a mean chocolate chip."

"Let's go!" Darcy grabbed his arm and they rushed off.

Stephanie started toward the cookie table, too. "Let's hurry before they're all gone," she suggested.

Luke touched her shoulder to stop her. "Hold on—I want to ask you something." Stephanie paused, surprised, waiting to see what he'd say.

"Skip breakfast tomorrow," Luke said. "And meet me down at the lake."

"What?" Stephanie laughed.

"Come on. Just do it," Luke said. "Promise me. I'll meet you at seven forty-five. You can run into the dining room and grab something to eat."

"Okay," Stephanie said. "Well, um, where? The beach, or—"

"I'll find you," Luke promised. "Just be there."

What is he planning? Stephanie wondered, studying Luke's sly grin. She had no idea what it could be—but she couldn't wait to find out!

CHAPTER
8

◆ ◢ ◆ ◆

Stephanie hurried down to the lake early Wednesday morning. She wanted to see Luke and make sure she was back in time for her sailing class. She couldn't get into trouble today—not with the CIT contest starting that afternoon. She had a feeling Heather would be grading her on practically *everything*—even on how neatly her sneakers were tied and whether she knew the Sail-Away chant by heart.

Stephanie slipped on her sport sunglasses when she got to the lake. The morning sun was very bright. She glanced around the beach for Luke but didn't see him anywhere.

She heard a motorboat on the water and

walked out to the docks to take a look. As it neared the dock, Stephanie's heart beat faster. Luke was driving the boat—and it was roaring straight for the dock.

Just when Stephanie thought he was going to crash, he steered abruptly to the left and cut the motor. The speedboat bobbed up and down in its own wake, the inboard engine sputtering.

"Good morning," Luke said with a smile.

"Luke!" Stephanie said with a laugh. "You scared me half to death."

"I did?" Luke grinned. "Good."

Stephanie shook her head. "I can't believe you."

"Hop in. We don't have much time," Luke said.

"We're going for a boat ride?" Stephanie asked.

"Sure, why not?"

Stephanie thought she remembered something in the camp rules about only counselors being allowed to drive motorboats. But she wasn't sure. If she said something, Luke would probably think she was a complete wimp. "Are you sure it's okay?" she asked.

"It's fine. We'll be back before anyone even knows we're gone," Luke promised. "Hop in! I have an extra life jacket right here."

Stephanie grabbed the side of the boat. "I don't know. Should we really do this?"

"Stephanie. Are you telling me you're *afraid* to go out in a boat?" Luke asked.

"No, of course not," Stephanie said. *Well, maybe just a little,* she admitted to herself. *But the fact that he's so cute is probably going to sway my decision.*

"Then, get in," Luke said. "I was a CIT last summer, and I know how to drive a motorboat."

Stephanie glanced back at the boathouse and at shore. *Should I do this? Why not?* she decided. *What do I have to lose?* She dropped her towel on the dock. Then she held the side of the boat and climbed in. "You have to get me back by eight-thirty," she warned. "I have to be on time for my sailing class."

"No problem." Luke handed her the life jacket. Stephanie fastened it tightly before Luke started the motor again. "Ready?" he asked her.

Stephanie nodded. "Ready."

"Here comes your tour of Lake Clearwater," Luke said. He turned the key, pressed a button, and the boat edged away from the dock. They gradually gained speed as they crossed the lake.

"Hey, do you water-ski?" he asked Stephanie.

She shook her head. "I've never done it before. I

don't know how." Her hair blew behind her in the breeze. She'd never gone so fast in a boat before, either!

"You're kidding!" Luke said. "Some time this summer, I'll teach you how." He ran a hand through his thick blond hair.

Sometime this summer. He makes it sound like we'll be spending a lot of time together, Stephanie thought.

"I'd teach you right now, but we don't have time," Luke said. "How come you're so worried about being back by eight-thirty?"

Stephanie rolled her eyes. "Well . . . first of all, I have this CIT in my cabin—"

"I thought *you* were a CIT," Luke commented.

"Not yet," Stephanie told him. "But my big problem right now is that I have this CIT who is out to get me. I'm not exactly fond of her, either—but I'd never go out of my way to be mean to her. And since I'm not a CIT—yet—she's totally holding it over my head that she is. She keeps looking for all these mistakes I've supposedly made. So if she found out I was doing anything I shouldn't be, like waterskiing—"

"You'd be in hot water." Luke nodded. "I get it. So how can you still become a CIT? Those jobs are all taken, right?"

"They were," Stephanie said. "But a girl broke her leg yesterday, so there's an opening. I have to compete with someone else for the job, starting this afternoon."

"Compete? *Why?* As if they could find someone better," Luke scoffed.

Stephanie laughed. "Thanks."

He steered the boat into a secluded cove. A few small motorboats were idling there. Fishermen had cast lines into the water.

"How long have you been coming to Camp Clearwater?" Stephanie asked.

"A really long time. In fact, I live close by all year," Luke said. "See those houses across the lake? That light blue one with the really long dock is ours."

"Wow! You're so lucky," Stephanie told him. "You get to live on the lake year-round?"

"It's definitely cool," Luke said.

"If you live in town, why don't you just stay there during the summer? Doesn't Clearwater have any day campers?" Stephanie asked.

"Nope. And besides, I started coming here because my parents travel a lot in the summer," Luke said as they reached the other end of the lake. "When I was a kid, there was no way I wanted to go to Europe when I could swim and ski all summer. I know that probably sounds really dumb *now,* but—"

"Not really," Stephanie said. "I definitely understand. That's why I really want that waterfront CIT job—so I can spend all summer on the lake."

"I'm sure you'll get it," Luke said. "Why would they pick someone else over you, when you can right a canoe in under two seconds?"

Stephanie grinned. "Thanks." Luke drove the motorboat back up toward the camp. When he got fairly close, Stephanie asked him to stop. "I'll swim from here," she said.

"You sure? It's kind of a long way," Luke said.

"I'm in shape—I can do it," Stephanie told him. *Besides, I don't want anyone to see me cruise up to the dock in a motorboat! Just in case there's anything wrong about this. . . .*

Luke cut the motor. Everything was suddenly quiet. They were drifting with the current.

He touched her shoulder. "Listen," he said. "Do you have a free afternoon this week?"

Stephanie looked up at him. "Sure," she replied. "This Friday."

"Great. I'm free then, too." Luke slid his sunglasses down the bridge of his nose and looked Stephanie in the eye. "What do you say we do something fun? Something really exciting . . ."

Stephanie gazed into Luke's bright green eyes. *Is he asking me for a date?* "What did you have in mind?" she asked.

"You'll see. Meet me at Clearwater at one o'clock Friday."

"Come on," Stephanie prodded. "At least give me a little hint—"

Luke flashed her a grin. "No hints. That would ruin the surprise. But I promise you, it will be an adventure. You're not afraid, are you?"

Stephanie's skin tingled with excitement. What could he be planning for her? "I'm not afraid," she insisted. "I'll see you Friday." She waved at Luke, then perched on the edge of the boat, preparing to dive into the water.

"Wait!" Luke rushed up behind Stephanie and put his hands on her waist. He pulled her toward him.

Stephanie glanced over her shoulder at Luke. She could feel his breath on the back of her neck. What was he doing?

"You forgot to take off the life jacket," Luke said. He unclipped the belt from her waist.

"Oh. Right." Stephanie felt her face redden. He only wanted the life jacket. But if that was all he wanted, why was he still holding her?

Luke cleared his throat and stepped away. "See you Friday."

Stephanie smiled at him. "Thanks again for the ride." She quickly dove into the lake. When she surfaced, she started taking short, strong strokes through the cold morning water toward shore. She glanced over her shoulder at Luke once and saw that he was watching her.

This is so weird, Stephanie thought. *I feel so comfortable with Luke—but nervous at the same time. I never know what he's thinking. But whenever I'm with him, he makes everything seem so exciting.* There was something mysterious about Luke—and this was one mystery Stephanie couldn't wait to solve!

About ten minutes later she reached one of the docks. She climbed the ladder on the end and stepped onto the wooden planks. To her surprise, Kayla was standing there.

"Stephanie! What did you do, swim across the lake?" she asked.

"Just about!" Stephanie grabbed her towel off the dock and wrapped it around her waist. She turned to look out at the water. Luke had just fired up the motor. He was cruising back toward the boys' camp. Stephanie caught his eye and waved to him. He honked the horn in reply.

"Was that Luke?" Kayla asked.

Stephanie smiled as she squeezed water out of her hair. "We went for a little ride and then I swam back to shore."

"You guys were riding around in a camp motorboat?" Kayla asked.

"It's no big deal. We knew what we were doing," Stephanie said. "At least, Luke did. He used to be a CIT—"

"Only counselors are allowed to drive the boats," Kayla said. "You broke camp rules. You should be careful, Steph. Especially with this CIT job on the line."

"Don't worry," Stephanie said. "You're the only one who saw me. Nobody else is going to find out. And I promise, I won't do it again!"

"Steph, we're not the only ones down here," Kayla said. "There are other people in the boathouse—it's almost eight-thirty!"

"Oh." Stephanie bit her lip. "Who's in there?"

"Terri and Julia," Kayla said. "And Rene and Darah."

Stephanie grimaced. "I guess I was out on the

boat longer than I thought. I didn't know we were going for a ride when we made the plan to meet—"

"So he planned this?" Kayla asked. "I think that was totally irresponsible of him—"

"Don't blame it all on Luke!" Stephanie insisted. "I wanted to go. It's not like he forced me." *Of course, he did sort of dare me,* she added to herself.

"I know he's cute, and you like him a lot," Kayla said. "But—"

"Who's cute?" Rene dumped about ten canoe paddles onto the dock. Darah was right behind her. She had ten more paddles under her arm.

Stephanie turned around. When did Rene get there? Had she seen Stephanie and Luke together? *Oh, no,* Stephanie thought. *I'm doomed.*

"It's not that Luke guy you were talking to last night, is it?" Darah asked.

"Actually, it is," Stephanie said. "Do you have a problem with that?"

Rene distributed the paddles into the canoes tied to the dock. "Stephanie, about Luke," she said. "I heard he's bad news."

"Oh, really?" Stephanie asked. She wasn't about to take Rene's word on anything.

"Jenny was talking about him at the movie last

night," Rene went on. "Because everyone *knows* he switched the movies."

"No, he didn't," Stephanie said.

"That's not what I heard," Darah said. "He's major trouble. That's why he's not a counselor again this year."

"That's not true," Stephanie said. Though Luke hadn't actually said why he wasn't a CIT this summer. *There has to be another reason*, she thought.

"Stephanie, don't take this the wrong way," Rene went on. "But as your CIT, I'm going to give you some advice."

Stephanie rolled her eyes. "I can't wait."

"Quit spending so much time with Luke—or you'll get in trouble, too," Rene said.

"So much time?" Stephanie asked. "I just met him. I've talked to him like . . . once." *Okay, so it was three times, and we have a date planned for Friday. But she doesn't need to know that. Maybe Rene is trying to scare me off so she can go out with Luke herself.*

"Listen to me, Stephanie." Rene curled her hair around her ear. "Luke had some problems last summer."

"Excuse me, but were you *here* last summer?"

Stephanie asked. "Because I thought you were traveling in Europe and then taking the Super Summer Adventure trip."

"Look." Rene gritted her teeth. "I heard Heather and Jenny's dad talking. They were saying something about how they hoped he was going to straighten out this year. I thought you'd like to know that you should stay away from him. But excuse me for trying to do the right thing." Rene turned on her heel and marched back toward the boathouse.

"She's only trying to help," Darah said. "Go ahead. Hang out with Luke all you want—we don't care. But you might just get into trouble *with* him next time." She followed Rene up the beach.

Stephanie glanced at Kayla and shrugged. "What do they know? Anyway, I should get going—Anita's probably looking for me for sailing class."

Kayla nodded. "Stephanie—before you go, I want to say something. For once, I think the Flamingoes might be right. Watch out for Luke."

CHAPTER
9

◆ ◀ ◈ ◆

"Are you girls ready?" Heather was standing on the steps of the lodge Wednesday afternoon, her clipboard in one hand and a whistle on a string around her neck.

"I am," Stephanie said as she tightened the band around her ponytail.

Tiffany pulled up her white socks. "I think I am," she said.

"Great. Then, let's get started." Heather put the whistle between her lips and blew it.

Stephanie cringed at the ear-splitting sound. Was she supposed to salute or something?

"Testing. One, two, three, testing!" Heather yelled.

Both Tiffany and Stephanie leaped back. Heather's yell was almost as loud as the whistle.

Heather consulted her clipboard. "Tiffany Schroder?" she asked.

"Um . . . present?" Tiffany said.

Heather made a large check. "Stephanie Tanner?"

"Here," Stephanie said. Wasn't that obvious?

Tiffany looked at Stephanie with her eyebrows raised. Stephanie almost burst out laughing. If she and Tiffany ever did bond as friends, it would be because of the way Heather was running this contest.

Heather made another check. "Since everyone is present and accounted for, it looks like we're ready to start. Forward, march—"

The screen door to the lodge banged open. Jenny rushed outside with a dish towel in her hands. "Oh, good! I'm not too late."

"Too late?" Heather asked.

"Yeah! I was afraid when I got stuck with dish duty that I'd miss the whole thing." Jenny finished drying her hands and set the dish towel on the log railing. "So, where do we start?"

"We?" Heather shook her head. "I don't know what you're talking about. How are you involved in this?"

"Jenny's helping you run the contest!" Tiffany said cheerfully.

"What?" Stephanie muttered as she looked at Tiffany. That couldn't be fair.

"Dad said you might need some help," Jenny said. "I offered to pitch in, and he said okay."

Jenny isn't doing this because Heather needs help, Stephanie thought. *She's doing it because Tiffany does!*

"He didn't mention anything about this to me," Heather said. She checked the pager clipped to the waistline of her khaki shorts. "No calls. No notes. Are you sure he said it was all right?"

Jenny shifted from one foot to the other. "Well, he said if *you* said it was okay—"

"Ah—I see." Heather pulled her baseball cap more tightly onto her head. "I'm sorry, Jenny. But I think I can handle this on my own. And I'm sure you have more important things to do—like go down to the stables and coach riding?"

"But I really want to help," Jenny said with a pout. "And my dad *said*—"

"I'll make you a deal," Heather offered. "You let me run part one of the test here today. Tomorrow, maybe you can help with part two. In the meantime, why don't you set a good example and run off to help your campers? I'm sure *they* need you more than I do."

Jenny nodded. "Okay. I guess you're right. Well, good luck, Tiffany," she said.

Heather cleared her throat. "Ahem. We have two contestants here?"

"Oh, and, um, good luck to you, too, Stephanie!" Jenny added. She grabbed the dish towel off the railing and vanished into the lodge.

Heather made a note on her clipboard and then looked up at Stephanie and Tiffany. "Before we begin, I thought I'd let you know what we're looking for in a counselor."

"But we want to be only counselors in training," Tiffany said.

"Yes. Correct." Heather smiled. "But you must also want to be a counselor . . . and that's why you're *training* to be one. Right?"

"Oh. Oh!" Tiffany giggled. "Right."

Darcy was right, Stephanie thought. *Tiffany doesn't know what being a CIT means!* This competition was going to be easy.

"We expect a lot from our counselors, junior counselors, and CITs," Heather began. "They—you—must all meet the same standard of excellence. That includes, but is not limited to, being prompt, reliable, responsible, cheerful, able to handle any emergency, pleasant to everyone, with a positive attitude and a love for the outdoors."

Stephanie nodded. "I think I meet that description."

"Me, too," Tiffany quickly piped up. "For sure."

"We'll see. Inside, girls!" Heather opened the screen door. "Don't forget to wipe your feet. Follow me to the kitchen!"

Stephanie and Tiffany stopped behind Heather. They were standing in front of two giant stainless refrigerators. "What are we doing in here?" Tiffany asked.

Stephanie was wondering the same thing. Since when did CITs have to cook?

"We'll begin the indoor part of the test with some lodge skills. These may seem trivial, but you never know what you'll be called upon to do." Heather pointed to the giant cabinet by the window. "As you know, that's where we keep all the silverware and plates. CITs aren't always in charge of setting tables—in fact, it's usually a camper's job. But I've decided to time each of you setting a complete table for ten."

"Complete?" Tiffany asked. "What does that mean?"

"Silverware, plates, napkins, glasses . . ." Heather ran through a checklist on her clipboard. "That should do it."

"How are we going to carry—"

Heather waved her index finger in the air. "No, no, no! No talking it over or asking for help!" she scolded. "You need to be able to think on your feet. We'll flip a coin to see who goes first."

A table for ten? Stephanie almost laughed. *That's what I have to do a couple of nights a week at home.* With her large extended family, Stephanie was used to this particular chore—a little *too* used to it.

Heather tossed a coin into the air. Stephanie called heads, and won the toss. That meant Tiffany had to go first. Stephanie was getting a really good feeling about this contest.

She watched as Tiffany tried to set the table. It took her nearly ten minutes, and she forgot a few items. Stephanie set the table in five and did it perfectly.

"Round one—Stephanie," Heather declared. "And maybe a bonus point or two for neatness. Very nice. Not a knife out of place."

"That's not fair! You didn't say there would be bonus points," Tiffany complained.

"Don't worry, Tiffany—I know you'll earn

some, too. Now, the next task is a real challenge." Heather handed both of them aprons. "Put these on, and each of you grab a stove—not literally. That could be painful." She laughed. "Gee, I am really on a roll today. Not that kind of roll." She pointed to a bag of leftover rolls on the counter. "Okay, okay, enough jokes."

Tiffany raised her eyebrows again at Stephanie. Stephanie smiled as she tied the red apron around her waist.

"I think I like Heather the army sergeant better than Heather the comedian," Stephanie mumbled as she and Tiffany toured the supply closet.

"Me, too," Tiffany agreed.

"Are you two talking? That's not allowed." Heather stood between them like a wall. "Okay. Are you ready?"

"Sure," Stephanie replied.

"Here's the challenge. Use whatever supplies you need—in moderation, just so I can see what your plan is," Heather said. "The cook has called in sick. All the counselors are on an overnight trip, so *you* need to make breakfast for a hundred hungry campers. Ready and . . . go!"

"Hold on!" Tiffany called. "Where are the counselors? I mean, how can they all be gone at once?"

"They just are," Heather said.

"But that wouldn't happen, so . . . anyway, why wouldn't you or Mr. McCready cook?" Tiffany asked.

"Because that's not our job," Heather replied sternly. "And because I just asked you to do it. So get started."

Stephanie had to agree with Tiffany. This challenge didn't make much sense. But if Heather wanted to assess their problem-solving skills, that was okay with her.

Tiffany stared at the stove. "A hundred hungry people. I know!" She turned to Heather. "We could order takeout."

Heather shook her head. "The closest takeout would be twenty minutes away. And you don't have a car."

"They'd deliver!" Tiffany said. "For a hundred people. Are you kidding?"

"You don't have the money to order a hundred breakfasts," Heather reasoned. "Do you?"

"Okay, then. Good point. I *so* don't want to spend my summer allowance on breakfast." Tiffany grabbed a giant box of pancake mix off the shelf and rushed out to the stove. She fiddled with the dials until she turned on the griddle.

Then she started to dump pancake mix into a bowl and add water.

"Stephanie, why aren't you cooking?" Heather asked after Tiffany had poured scoops of batter onto the griddle.

"Because I'm going to feed everyone fresh fruit and cold cereal," Stephanie said. "I was trying to think if there's anything else I could serve with that, but I guess I'll go ahead and start bringing it out."

"Rats! Why didn't I think of that?" Tiffany complained as she wielded a spatula above the grill. "Stop spreading!" she yelled at the batter.

"Brilliant idea," Heather congratulated Stephanie. "Round two goes to Steph—"

"Hold on! I'm making pancakes and they're almost done," Tiffany said. "So why don't I win?"

Heather stared at the griddle. "For one thing, you have one giant pancake there. And for another, you forgot to oil the griddle first."

A burning smell filled the kitchen as Tiffany struggled to flip the mega-pancake. After trying for a few minutes, she threw her spatula down in defeat. "Round two. Stephanie," she conceded. "Rene's going to kill me."

Stephanie couldn't help but feel great about the

way the afternoon was going. At this rate, she was going to win every event. Then she'd have such a huge lead, there would be no way Tiffany could catch her.

"Let's head for my cabin," Heather said. "I've got a bed-making race for you to start with—all eight bunk beds, mind you, top and bottom. Then we'll move to bathroom cleaning."

"Ugh," Tiffany muttered under her breath.

"I agree," Stephanie mumbled back.

"By the way. You two *do* know how to make a hospital corner, don't you?" Heather asked on her way out of the Lodge.

Tiffany gave her a blank look. "A hospital corner? Is that like . . . driving fast or something? Because it's an emergency?"

"It's something about the way you fold the sheet when you make the bed," Stephanie told her.

"Oh, great," Tiffany muttered.

Somehow I see myself winning Rounds Three and Four, Stephanie thought as she cheerfully followed Heather. *And then the rest of the contest!*

Stephanie Tanner, CIT. It has a nice ring to it.

CHAPTER
10

◆ ◀ ◆ ◆

"Stephanie! Wake up, wake up!"

Stephanie slowly opened her eyes. *Where am I? Who's shaking me?* Rene's face slowly came into focus. "Wh—what's going on?" she sleepily mumbled.

"Stephanie, it's an emergency. Get dressed and come with me!" Rene said.

"What emergency? Is everyone okay?" Stephanie sat up and glanced at the alarm clock beside her bed. It was almost midnight—it was almost *Thursday!* "Is there a fire?"

"No—everyone's fine," Rene said as she pulled a cap over her head. "But you won't be if you don't get up right now."

"Why?" Stephanie asked. *What is Rene talking about?*

"It's part of the contest. It was Heather's idea," Rene whispered urgently. "She told us *all* to be down at the lake at midnight."

"She . . . she did?" Stephanie rubbed her eyes. "When?"

"Just now! She came by," Rene said. "It's for all CITs. Part of our emergency response training or something like that." Rene zipped up her fleece jacket. "She talked so fast, I barely heard what she said. Come on, Stephanie—get out of bed or you'll miss the whole thing. We're the last ones—I already saw Darcy and Anna go by."

Emergency response training? Okay. Sure. Stephanie hadn't heard of anything like that, but she swung her legs over the edge of her bunk bed. She looked sleepily around the cabin. Leah was fast asleep—and so was everyone else! "Where's Julia?" she asked.

"Tonight's her night off—she won't be back until one o'clock, remember?" Rene explained. "Are you ready?"

"I don't know. Should we leave with everyone here asleep?" Stephanie quickly threw on a pair of jeans and a sweatshirt.

"Stephanie, everyone in this cabin is at least thirteen. They'll be *fine*. We'll be right back!" Rene said.

"Okay." Stephanie slipped her feet into her sandals and met Rene at the door. "The lake?" she asked. "Are you sure?"

"I'm sure," Rene said. "Come on, I have a flashlight. You go first and I'll be right behind you. That way you can see where you're going."

Stephanie glanced quickly at Rene. *Why is she being so nice to me?* she wondered. Then she started running down the path to the lake. The sky was cloudy, so no stars were visible. Even the moon was hidden behind a large cloud.

"Faster!" Rene urged.

"I can hardly *see*," Stephanie called over her shoulder. "Shine the flashlight up ahead of me."

"I am," Rene said. "The batteries must be dying or something."

Stephanie thought it was strange that she didn't see or hear anyone else rushing down to the lake. *We must be really late!* She turned on the speed.

Suddenly the light behind Stephanie went out. She couldn't see where she was going. "Rene? Did the battery die?" Stephanie held her arms out in front of her to make sure she didn't bump into anything. "Rene?" Stephanie turned around, stumbled a few times as she tripped on a stone— and crashed right into a fir tree!

She plucked prickly needles out of her hair and stared at the empty path behind her. Rene—and the flashlight—had vanished.

What happened to her? Stephanie wondered. She turned back around and tried to head in the direction of the lake. *Rene probably took a shortcut so she could beat me there*, Stephanie thought. *That way she'll look good and I'll look bad. But I can't give up that easily—I have to get to the lake as soon as I can!*

Stephanie kept running. She held her hands in front of her to make sure she didn't bump into any more trees. A minute later she reached the beach. She stumbled around for a few moments, looking for her friends. Then she looked for Rene and Tiffany and Heather. Even though the night was pitch-black, it was obvious no one else was there.

It's a trick, Stephanie suddenly realized. She couldn't believe she hadn't seen through Rene's story before. *Rene did this as a prank!*

Stephanie jogged back to her cabin as fast as

she could. It was hard because of the darkness. She had to watch every step she took. She didn't want to trip and end up with a broken ankle like Suzanne. *That's probably what Rene had in mind. She can't stand the idea that I might be a CIT, too.*

Stephanie stopped in front of her cabin, out of breath. She couldn't wait to tell Rene off for the stupid prank she'd pulled.

But when she got closer, she saw Julia standing in the doorway, her arms folded across her chest. "Stephanie! Where have you been?" she asked.

Stephanie gulped. Now she was in trouble! "I— uh—was at the lake," she said.

"You were? Why?" Julia demanded.

Rene appeared in the cabin doorway behind Julia. "She snuck down there to see her new boyfriend, Luke Hayes."

"What?" Stephanie shook her head. "No, I didn't. I went down there only because *you* told me I was supposed to be at the lake for a CIT drill."

"What CIT drill?" Julia looked at Rene. Then she turned back to Stephanie. "Luke Hayes is your boyfriend? What's going on, you two?"

Rene and Stephanie glared at each other in silence.

"Okay, I see we need to have a conference. Rene, close the door behind you—we've disturbed everyone's sleep enough already," Julia said, stepping outside.

"We want to hear the argument!" Leah called out as Rene shut the door.

"Let's sit over here." Julia perched on a rock several yards from the cabin.

Rene sat on a rock opposite Stephanie.

"So who wants to tell me what really happened?" Julia asked. "And no lying—I want the truth."

"I told you. Stephanie had a date with Luke planned—"

"I did not!" Stephanie protested. "Rene woke me up and dragged me down there by saying it was this last-minute CIT drill Heather came up with. I'm in that contest with Tiffany, remember? Next thing I know, Rene takes off—with the flashlight. And it turns out there was no drill!"

"You weren't supposed to go all the way," Rene said. "It's not my fault you didn't realize you were being tricked."

"She just confessed," Stephanie said to Julia. "She just admitted she was trying to get me in trouble!"

91

"Yes, she did. That's what I asked for—honesty. And I can understand a little friendly rivalry. It wouldn't be the first practical joke I'd seen between campers, and I'm sure it won't be the last," Julia said. "However, that doesn't mean you should get off without being punished, Rene."

"*Me?* How about punishing *her?*" Rene said. "She went out in a motorboat from Clearwater with a guy who's not even supposed to be driving one!"

Stephanie's jaw dropped. *So she did see me. And she's been waiting to use the information against me—until now!*

"Stephanie? Is that true?" Julia asked.

"Well, um . . . I guess he wasn't *technically* allowed to drive a motorboat—I mean, a Clearwater one. But I didn't know that! And I never planned on going for a ride," Stephanie said.

"Planned or not." Julia fixed Stephanie with a serious gaze. "Did you take a ride in a motorboat with someone other than a counselor?"

Stephanie nodded. "But it was safe—I wore a life jacket! And he used to be a CIT—"

Julia shook her head. "CITs can't drive motorboats, Stephanie. And Luke Hayes isn't even a CIT."

"I didn't know only counselors could drive the boats," Stephanie said. "I really didn't—not until I got back to shore. When I found out, I felt awful."

"Not awful enough to turn yourself in," Rene said.

"I wasn't going to do it again!" Stephanie said.

Julia looked up at the dark sky for a minute. "I really don't know what to do here. Obviously you guys don't get along. And you've known each other for years, so that's not likely to change anytime soon." She let out a deep sigh. "But you can't keep pulling stunts like tonight, Rene—not if you want to stay a CIT, and be a counselor someday. And, Stephanie, you can't break camp rules—period. Whether you make it as a CIT or not."

Stephanie nodded. "I understand."

"So do I," Rene said.

"I'm not going to punish you this time. But I have to warn you both," Julia said. "If anything like this happens again—and I mean anything at all—I'll tell Mr. McCready about it. You'll both have to deal with him then. I know he's not half as understanding about breaking rules as I am."

"Fine," Rene said as she got to her feet.

"Fine," Stephanie added.

The only way I can get back at Rene for getting me into trouble tonight is by becoming a CIT, Stephanie thought as she headed into the cabin for bed. *She'll hate that.*

So that's what I'm going to do!

CHAPTER
11

◆ ◀ ◆ ◆

Stephanie ran up to the outdoor skills course on Thursday afternoon and stopped short. Heather and Tiffany were sitting on the rope bridge. Jenny was standing behind them. She was looking over Heather's shoulder at the clipboard.

"Okay, so today's plan starts here and ends down at the lake, right?" Jenny asked.

Stephanie cleared her throat. "Um, hello?"

Heather looked up at Stephanie. "Good morning, Stephanie! You were very nearly late. Ready for action?"

"That depends. What is *she* doing here?" Stephanie asked as she stared at Jenny.

"Heather needs my help," Jenny answered. "Well, should we get started?"

More like Tiffany needs your help, Stephanie thought. *To keep me from winning and becoming a CIT.*

"Excellent. I thought we could begin with a balancing test," Heather said. "Jenny, please stay out of the way—in fact, stand at the other end if you don't mind. Tiffany, Stephanie—I want you to walk the length of that narrow beam." Heather pointed to the lowest one on the course—it was only a few feet off the ground.

Stephanie was puzzled. "Excuse me, Heather," she said. "But what does having good balance have to do with being a CIT?"

"Counselors need to demonstrate fitness in all areas," Heather replied sharply. "Are you ready?"

Tiffany adjusted a pink barrette in her bangs. "Can I go first?"

"Sure," Stephanie said. She wanted to win this event—no matter how silly it seemed. "Be my guest." *Maybe Jenny will try to interfere. But all I have to do is win one event—and the competition is over! Tiffany can't catch me now.*

Stephanie gawked at Tiffany as she practically ran down the beam. At the end she leaped off and threw her arms over her head. "I am *so* glad I learned the balance beam last year in gymnastics," Tiffany said.

"Excellent job! No falls, and you did it in record time," Heather said.

"Perfect ten!" Jenny cheered.

"Stephanie, your turn!" Heather said. "Begin!"

Stephanie stepped onto the beam carefully. *This is going to be easy*, she told herself. She held her arms out and started down the beam.

"Oh, no!" Jenny suddenly ran right toward Stephanie. She waved her hands in the air. "Look out!"

"What?" Stephanie wobbled back and forth on the beam—then lost her balance and hopped onto the ground. "What was that all about?"

"There was a bee flying around your head!" Jenny said. "Shoo!"

"Jenny!" Stephanie yelled. "How could you do that?"

"Do what?"

"There's no bee! And even if there was, so what? It wouldn't sting me," Stephanie said.

"It might. And you're allergic—aren't you?" Jenny asked. "I thought I remembered that from last summer."

"I'm *not*," Stephanie said. She turned to Heather. "Can I get back on and start over?"

"Certainly, Stephanie," Heather replied. "And this time, Jenny, try to keep quiet."

Jenny came to stand by Heather. "I was only trying to help," she said. *"Honest."*

I don't think the Flamingoes know the meaning of the word honest, Stephanie thought.

"Okay, Stephanie," Heather said. "Give it another shot."

Stephanie stepped onto the balance beam again. She held her arms out—and walked carefully down the beam.

"Good," Heather said when Stephanie jumped off. Heather looked at her stopwatch. "But not good enough. Tiffany is the winner—by one and a half seconds!"

Jenny shot Stephanie a triumphant glance. *Don't look too happy,* Stephanie thought. *It's not over yet.*

"Attention, girls!" Heather said. "Our next event is a fitness test. I want you to sprint from here to the lodge and back. I'll time you."

"That whole way?" Tiffany said.

"It's not even half a mile there and back," Jenny said. "Don't sweat it! Heather, I'll run the stopwatch," she volunteered. "You know, in case you need to make more plans for the next couple of events."

"That's a great idea," Heather said. "Here. When I blow the whistle, Tiffany, start running."

Stephanie cleared her throat. "Heather, I don't mean to be critical, but, um . . . shouldn't all these outdoor events take place on the waterfront?"

"Not at all. Because you never know what you'll be asked to do. I'm interested in getting the best all-around candidate. But we'll get to the water—don't worry," Heather said. "Ready, Tiffany, and—"

"How come I have to go first?" Tiffany asked.

"Just do it," Jenny urged her.

Heather started the race and Tiffany sprinted down the path. *I wish I had worn a watch today!* Stephanie thought as they all waited for Tiffany. *I bet she doesn't even go the whole way!*

"Is there someone there checking to make sure we actually reach the lodge?" Stephanie asked.

"Oh, yes. There's a counselor checkpoint," Heather said.

When Tiffany came back, Jenny noted her time on the clipboard. "Great job! Stephanie's next."

"Can you tell me the time to beat?" Stephanie

asked. She tried to look at the clipboard. She could at least count the seconds in her head.

"Sorry—that wouldn't be fair." Jenny shrugged. "Ready?"

Stephanie ran down the path at top speed. She wasn't going to lose to Tiffany! When she reached the lodge, she saw Julia sitting on the steps.

"Go, Stephanie!" she called. "All you need to do is tag up and head back!"

A few drops of sweat trickled down Stephanie's back as she sprinted back up the trail. She felt like she was running faster than she ever had before.

"Congratulations!" Jenny said when Stephanie passed her.

"I won?" Stephanie panted. If she won this event, Tiffany wouldn't have a chance of catching her—she'd be too many points ahead. Unless of course Tiffany scored bonus points, which was highly unlikely.

"Um . . . let me see. I was actually just congratulating you for finishing." Jenny hit the stopwatch button.

"Wait—you should have gotten my finish time ten seconds ago!" Stephanie protested.

Jenny gave her an annoying smile. "I did. I

was just checking. Tiffany beat you by twelve seconds."

"What?" Stephanie said.

"So Tiffany wins the sprint," Heather said. "Now, the next event—" There was a loud beeping sound. "Oh, rats, I'm being paged." She looked at the pager on her belt and read the brief voice-mail message. "It's an emergency at the laundry. One of the lint filters is clogged. I'd better run and check it out."

"Can't it wait?" Stephanie asked.

"Oh, no. There's a risk of fire," Heather said. "But hold on, I'll be right back. Jenny, perhaps you could administer the next event. Head to the waterfront and start the swim contest. The markers are already placed. I'll meet you there!" She shoved the clipboard at Jenny and ran off down the trail.

"Okay, guys—change into your suits and meet me at the lake!" Jenny said. "Gee, I *do* hope Heather will be able to join us." She and Tiffany started giggling.

Stephanie glared at them. She'd actually felt a little sorry for Tiffany at the beginning of the contest. But now that she and Jenny were cheating, her sympathy for Tiffany disappeared. "I should have known you'd fix the contest!" she shouted.

"I don't know what you're talking about," Tiffany said as she swept past Stephanie. "Can I help it if there's a . . . lint epidemic?"

"Just accept it," Jenny said. "Tiffany's good at some things!"

Yeah—like cheating! Stephanie thought as she raced for her cabin.

"This isn't fair!" Stephanie complained as she drifted across the finish line. "My oarlock broke. I had only one oar!"

Jenny shrugged. "Sorry."

"You must have been using an incorrect rowing technique," Heather said.

Stephanie glared at Jenny. Jenny was the one who'd assigned them their rowboats. Stephanie was convinced that she'd given her a defective one. *And Rene probably helped pick it out!*

It wouldn't have been so bad if she'd managed to win the swim race. But Jenny had caught her trying to make up extra time by not completely touching the dock when she turned around. She'd been disqualified!

This is so humiliating, Stephanie thought. *I lost every event today to Tiffany!*

"Well, girls, we have a tie score," Heather

announced. "Stephanie dominated yesterday, and Tiffany won today. Nice comeback, Tiffany!" Heather clapped her hands.

Stephanie was so angry, she could barely stand still. Couldn't Heather *see* that Jenny was helping Tiffany win every event? Didn't she realize that leaving Jenny in charge was completely unfair?

Tiffany pushed her wet bangs off her forehead and squeezed sweat out of her hair ribbon. "We don't have to have another day like this, do we?" she asked.

I hope not, Stephanie thought.

"Well . . ." Heather tapped her pen against the clipboard. "We do need to settle this right away."

"I know! We could draw straws, like Mr. McCready said," Tiffany suggested with a bright smile.

"No, no, that won't do. Not at all," Heather said.

Jenny looked at Tiffany and shrugged. "*I* thought it was a good idea," she told her.

Stephanie stepped closer to Heather. "What if we—"

"I know! I've got it," Heather cried. "We'll have a tiebreaker," Heather said.

Well, I kind of figured that, Stephanie thought. "What kind?"

"The kind that everyone can watch. On Saturday night, right before the big dance. In front of the entire camp, the boys' camp—it'll be a very exciting event, believe me!" Heather said proudly.

"Can't it be tomorrow?" Stephanie asked.

"Nope! You have your free afternoons and you need to stick to them, or it'll throw the whole schedule off," Heather said. "And on Saturday I have too many other tasks lined up during the day. It has to be Saturday night. And it has to be entertaining!"

"What is it?" Tiffany asked.

"I can't tell you." Heather fastened her pen to the clipboard. She put her whistle in her shorts pocket. "Take care, girls. I've got to go tell Mr. M. the exciting news. See you for the main event!" Heather gave a short laugh.

"Aren't you even going to give us a clue?" Tiffany begged.

"Yeah," Stephanie added. "How about a vague idea of what we should be ready for?"

"As you already know, being a CIT means being prepared for anything at any time," Heather said. "If I told you, that would defeat the whole purpose of the contest. Good-bye and good luck!" She headed down the beach and back toward the trail to the lodge.

"That did *not* sound good." Tiffany chewed her thumbnail. "Not at all!"

Jenny patted her on the back. "Don't worry. I'm sure it won't be that hard." She glanced at Stephanie. "And I think I know how I can make it easier."

"How? Are you going to cheat again?" Stephanie asked. She couldn't believe she had to be in an actual tiebreaker with Tiffany. She should have won every single event, *especially* at the waterfront!

And I would have—if Jenny hadn't been involved, Stephanie thought.

"We didn't cheat," Jenny said. "You just had a bad day, that's all."

"Yeah." Stephanie glared at her. "A *really* bad day."

Tiffany shrugged. "It happens to the best of us, you know." Then she and Jenny started giggling.

"Hi, girls—how was the contest?" Rene sauntered up onto the beach.

"Like you don't know," Stephanie said. "You obviously had Jenny fix the whole thing!"

"Are you crazy? Is the heat getting to you or something?" Jenny asked.

"Well, it *did* look like Stephanie was struggling," Rene said. "Your face is really red. I don't know if you're in good enough shape to be a CIT."

"I'm going to be a CIT," Stephanie told them all. "Your stupid plan isn't going to work. Just wait."

CHAPTER
12

◆ ◀ ◢ ◆

"I can't believe Jenny would be so obvious," Kayla said after Stephanie finished explaining the rest of the CIT contest on Friday at noon. Stephanie had met her friends on the porch outside the lodge after lunch. They were all sitting on or leaning against the railing and talking.

"That's horrible," Anna said. She rubbed at a red paint stain on her elbow. "How can she get away with stuff like that right under Heather's nose?"

"Because Heather wasn't there half the time," Stephanie explained. "She got called away because of an emergency. How much do you want to bet it was one of the Flamingoes who called her?"

"Don't worry, Stephanie—you'll still win," Darcy said. "I know it."

"Anyway, enough about the Flamingoes," Anna declared. "Let's talk about the fact that we have this afternoon completely to ourselves! What are you guys doing?"

Darcy grinned. "I'm going for a hike with Keith."

"You *are?*" Allie asked. "I'm so jealous!"

"I'm working on a special project," Anna said.

"Sounds mysterious," Stephanie commented. "Would this special project happen to have a name? And what does he look like?"

"It's not a *boy*," Anna said with a laugh.

"Then, what's the project?" Kayla asked.

"There's a girl in my cabin who's so homesick, she's miserable," Anna said. "I promised her we'd spend the afternoon making a giant painted card to send to her parents. Then we're riding a couple of the camp bikes down to the post office in town to mail it in person."

"That's nice of you," Darcy said.

Anna shrugged. "I'm feeling kind of homesick, too. I think I'll make a card for my parents at the same time." She smiled at Kayla. "How about you?"

"I'm going on a canoe trip, all around the lake, with a couple of friends," Kayla said. "We're going to explore the coves and look for wildlife. There are supposed to be loons and turtles here. Allie?"

"They need me at the stables, so I traded my day off. I'll be off tomorrow," Allie said. "Too bad. I was hoping we could go into town and check it out," she said to Stephanie.

"Oh. That sounds like fun, but actually, I have a date with Luke," Stephanie said. "He told me to meet him at one and to be ready for anything. Doesn't that sound exciting?"

"It actually sounds sort of risky," Darcy said as she traced the outline of a heart someone had carved into one of the porch beams.

"Why would you say that?" Stephanie asked.

"Because. I don't know Luke yet, but the times I've seen him, he's always doing something he shouldn't," Darcy said.

"Right," Kayla agreed. "Like climbing too high on the tightrope, or bombing around the lake in a camp motorboat when it's not allowed—"

"He's fun. He likes to take risks," Stephanie said. "That doesn't mean he's—"

"Dangerous?" Allie interrupted. "I don't know, Steph. I kind of think he is."

"Why?" Stephanie asked.

"You heard what Rene and Darah said about him getting into trouble last summer," Kayla reminded her.

Stephanie shook her head. She wasn't going to listen to any Flamingo rumors about Luke. "You guys just have the wrong impression of Luke. I can't wait for the dance tomorrow night—you guys can hang out with him then. And once you get to know him, you'll see what a nice guy he is."

Anna shrugged. "Okay. That sounds good to me. But if the 'anything' he was talking about includes something like rock climbing or hang gliding—make sure you wear a helmet."

Stephanie laughed. "It won't be *that* adventurous!"

The group broke up a few minutes later, and Stephanie said good-bye to her friends. She hurried to her cabin and quickly brushed her hair and changed into a clean T-shirt and cargo shorts. She pulled her hair back into a clip and checked her reflection in the mirror. *Not bad, considering all the running around I did this morning!* she thought.

She hurried along the path toward Camp Clearwater. She couldn't wait to see Luke! She entered the Camp Clearwater property through a wooden gate and headed straight for the boys' lodge. She was a few minutes early, but she hoped Luke would already be there.

As she reached the front steps, Luke's friend Max burst out of the lodge. "Hi, Max."

He grinned. His curly brown hair was covered by a red crusher hat, and he wore a Clearwater T-shirt and faded jean shorts. "Hi, Stephanie. What are you doing over here? Is it your afternoon off?" Max asked.

"Yeah. A couple of hours of freedom. I can't wait," Stephanie said. "Not that I mind being at camp—I didn't mean it that way."

"It's just cool to have a day where nothing's planned," Max said.

"Right," Stephanie agreed. "Hey, I'm supposed to meet Luke here. Have you seen him?"

Max's smile faded.

"Luke? Really? What are you guys doing?"

"I'm not sure," Stephanie said. "But knowing Luke, it'll be fun."

Max looked uncomfortable. "Stephanie, I don't know you very well, but I can tell you're a really nice person," he said.

"Oh? Well, thanks." Stephanie felt herself blush.

"And I don't want to interfere," Max went on. "But I wonder if you realize what kind of person Luke is. I think you should stay away from him."

Stephanie could hardly believe her ears. Why was everyone so determined to keep her and Luke apart? "Stay away from him?" she asked Max. "I thought you guys were friends. Why would you say something like that?"

"Because Luke is dangerous," Max said. "And you should know the truth about him."

Stephanie laughed wryly. "You make it sound like he's a criminal or something."

Max bit his lower lip. "Well . . . he sort of *is*."

CHAPTER
13

◆ ◀ ◆ ◆

"What?" Stephanie cried. "Come on. Luke is *not* a criminal."

"Well, not technically," Max admitted. "But that's only because they couldn't prove Luke was responsible."

Behind Stephanie, someone cleared his throat. "Did I just hear my name? Are you guys talking about me *again?*"

Stephanie whirled around. Luke!

Luke stood behind Stephanie, holding the handlebars of two brightly painted bicycles.

She glanced nervously at Max. What if Luke had heard Max talking about him? Max's face had turned bright red. He was clearly as embarrassed and uncomfortable as Stephanie.

"Actually," Stephanie began, "I was asking Max if he had seen you—"

Luke grinned. "I was only joking! I thought I heard my name, that's all."

"Oh. Right." Stephanie smiled at him.

"So, uh, where are you guys going?" Max asked.

"For a bike ride around the lake," Luke said. "I'm going to show Stephanie my family's house."

"We should get going—I have to be back by three," Stephanie said. "Which bike should I take?"

"This one should fit you. I can raise the seat if it's too short," Luke offered.

Stephanie climbed onto the bright yellow bike. It was an old cruiser-style bike with only three speeds. "It fits me fine. Where did you get it?" She smiled at Luke.

"The camp has a small bike shop—I work there a few afternoons a week," Luke said as he hopped onto the other bike. His was orange, and the seat looked about a hundred years old. The black leather was cracked and the springs were rusty. "Come on—let's go!"

Stephanie rode down the path behind Luke. A

few minutes later they came out on a dirt road that circled the lake. "We'll ride the easy way for a while—then I know a shortcut," Luke said. "So we can do some mountain biking."

"Sounds great!" Stephanie smiled at him. *Luke—a criminal? Why would Max say that?* She decided to push Max's comments out of her mind and enjoy the afternoon. If he had a grudge against Luke, that was his problem—not hers.

"How do you like riding these old clunkers?" Luke asked.

"Actually, they work pretty well," Stephanie said. "Considering they weigh about a million pounds." She laughed and shifted into second gear as they started up a long, steep hill.

Luke plunged off the dirt road onto a trail and hopped over a rock. Stephanie followed him. He rode fast and made a point of jumping over every obstacle in the way.

When they reached the small light-blue house about half an hour later, Luke got off the bike and leaned it against the porch. "So, here we are. Home sweet home."

Stephanie left her bike leaning against a tree. "Wow. This place is gorgeous. You have this whole end of the lake to yourselves, almost!" She peered through the kitchen window. "Anyone home?"

"No, my parents are away," Luke said. "But this woman Nancy stops by to check on the place once in a while. She's a friend of my mom's."

As he spoke, a tall, slim woman with short dark hair opened the door. "Luke!" she cried happily. "What are you doing here?"

"Stephanie, this is Nancy," Luke said. "I brought Stephanie by to show her the house."

"I'm glad I caught you," Nancy said. "I just stopped by to water the plants." She smiled at Stephanie and added, "It's nice to meet you."

"It's nice to meet you, too," Stephanie said. *If Luke's mom is anything like her friend*, Stephanie thought, *she must be pretty nice.*

Nancy picked up a watering can and started outside. "I'm going to water the plants on the porch," she told them. "Give a yell if you need anything."

Luke gave her a wave, then led Stephanie into the house. Inside it was light and airy, comfortably furnished with well-worn antiques.

"Here's what I wanted to show you," Luke said, opening the door to his room. He reached under his bed and pulled out a large black-bound book.

Stephanie took the book and opened it. It was filled with beautiful drawings and watercolors of the lake.

"Did you do these?" she asked.

Luke nodded. "I don't usually show them to my friends. Most guys aren't really interested in landscape drawing." Stephanie smiled, thinking he was probably trying to protect his daredevil image.

"But I wanted you to see them," he continued. "I wanted you to know I'm more than just a jock."

"They're wonderful," Stephanie said, touched that he would share them with her. *He's even more talented than I thought!* she realized.

He took the book back from her and replaced it under his bed. "Let's go out to the beach," he said.

As they passed through the den, Stephanie noticed a shelf full of trophies Luke had won for waterskiing and other sports.

"Hey, Luke . . . speaking of waterskiing, I heard that only counselors are allowed to drive the camp motorboats," Stephanie said casually.

"Oh. Yeah? Well, I guess that's right," Luke said.

"So you lied to me the other day when you said it was okay!" Stephanie said.

"Did I? Well, okay, maybe. But how else was I going to convince you to come with me?" Luke grinned, his green eyes sparkling.

"But we could have gotten in trouble," Stephanie said. "Don't you care?"

"I care about having fun. And sometimes that means doing things you're not supposed to," Luke said.

"But . . . if you really wanted to ride in a motorboat, why didn't you come here and get *that* one?" Stephanie asked. She pointed out the window at the motorboat floating just off-shore.

"No time. And actually . . . no keys. My dad takes those with him," Luke explained. "But even if he didn't, driving my own boat wouldn't be as much fun, because *that* wouldn't be against the rules. Come on outside."

Stephanie followed him down a stone path to the small beach. She walked out on his dock and gazed down the lake toward Camp Sail-Away. She could barely see it.

Luke came up beside her. "So, when are we going to water-ski?" he asked.

"I don't know," Stephanie said.

"Come on," Luke urged. "How about if we arrange for Charlie to take you out with me and Max one morning?"

Stephanie nodded. "I'd be up for that. Only . . . there's something about you and Max that I sort of don't understand."

"What's that?" Luke asked.

"How come you guys are so competitive? I mean—you don't really seem like friends. It's almost as if you don't like each other much." *In fact, he thinks you're a rotten person,* she thought to herself.

Luke adjusted a loose slat in the dock. "We used to be friends. Then I was a CIT last year and he wasn't, so I guess he was sort of jealous or something. Some other stuff happened." He shrugged. "I don't know."

"Oh." *What other stuff?* Stephanie wondered. *The stuff Darah and Rene were talking about?* "Like what?" she asked.

"It's not important. Hey—don't you need to be back at three?" Luke studied his watch.

Is he trying to dodge the question, or is it really time to go? Stephanie quickly checked her watch. "Oh, no! I have only twenty minutes to get back to camp—didn't it take us longer than that to get here?"

"No problem. Come on! I know another short-cut." Luke ran up the path. Nancy was just locking up the house. "See you later!" he called to her. "We've got to get back to camp."

"Have a good time!" Nancy called back.

Luke jumped on his bike. Stephanie was right behind him.

"We were supposed to do something adventurous today!" Luke said as they started riding. "All we did was sit around and talk. I meant to take you out in our kayak—teach you how to do some rolls."

"Sorry," Stephanie said as she pedaled along.

"Don't be. I'm not." Luke smiled at her. "Hey, I know—*this* will be our adventure. You've heard of time trials, right? Pretend we're racing for something. This is the Tour de Clearwater!"

I don't have to pretend! Stephanie thought desperately. *If I don't get back in time, Julia will have another mark against me.*

She pedaled even faster. They were almost halfway to camp when she heard a crack of thunder. Then the skies opened up and rain began to pour from the clouds above.

Luke started laughing. "Now it's really an adventure!" he yelled over the driving rain.

Stephanie laughed as they both raced down the slick road. The dirt road was rapidly turning into mud. Stephanie struggled to control her bike as she plowed ahead.

"We're here!" Luke pointed ahead to the wooden sign for Camp Sail-Away.

"What? I can't believe we made it so fast!" Stephanie said. They sprinted the last hundred yards uphill to the lodge, and she skidded to a stop. She climbed off the bike, laughing at her near fall. Her clothes were soaked through and water dripped from her shorts and T-shirt onto the ground.

Stephanie was about to hand her bike to Luke so he could take it back to the boys' camp, when her foot slipped in the mud. She started falling backward. She waved her arms to get her balance and started skidding right toward Luke.

"Whoa!" she cried out.

"I've got you!" Luke exclaimed, grabbing her arm to steady her. The bike crashed to the ground. He took both of her hands and pulled her close to him.

Stephanie looked up into his eyes as the rain fell all around them.

"You should probably go. Before you're late," Luke said.

"Yeah," Stephanie said. *But I don't want to leave—I want to stay right here.*

Luke put his hand on Stephanie's face and tipped her chin up toward him. Then he pressed his lips against hers in a soft, romantic kiss.

CHAPTER
14

Stephanie opened her eyes and gazed into Luke's. He smiled at her. She felt as if she'd melt into a puddle on the ground.

"I—I'd better go," she whispered. She turned and ran to her cabin. At the door, she paused to glance back at Luke. He was walking the two bikes back to Clearwater, splashing through the mud in the rain.

Stephanie ducked into her cabin and collapsed on her bed. *He kissed me!* she thought in amazement. *He actually kissed me!*

It had been an incredible day.

The next morning Stephanie couldn't think of anything but Luke. She went through all her normal camp activities twice as fast as usual. She couldn't wait for the day to be over—and for the boys' and girls' all-camp dance that night. First she'd win the tiebreaker—and then she'd get to see Luke.

I still can't believe we kissed yesterday, she thought as she and her friends got dressed for the dance.

"Hey, Steph—does this shirt go with this skirt?" Allie glanced down at her outfit.

"It goes fine," Stephanie told her. "But I think I have something that would look even better." She dug in her trunk and pulled out a flowered T-shirt. "How about this?"

"Awesome. I'll try it on," Allie said.

"So, do you have *any* idea what Heather has in mind for your tiebreaker?" Kayla fastened a necklace with small aquamarine rhinestones around her neck.

"Not at all," Stephanie said. "But she did say it would be indoors. That way everyone can watch."

"Maybe she's planning on having you arm-wrestle Tiffany for the job," Darcy joked.

"That would be fine with me," Stephanie said. "Because I'd win." She curled her arm and showed everyone her muscles.

"Okay, but what if Heather wants you and Tiffany to mud-wrestle?" Kayla joked.

"I just hope it's a fair fight," Anna said. "And that you come out ahead. We've spent the past three summers doing everything together. I don't want this one to be any different."

"You know what? I don't want to leave—even if I can't be a CIT," Stephanie said.

"Well, *duh*." Darcy put her arm around Stephanie's shoulders. "For one thing, you have a major crush on Luke. For another, you couldn't leave us even if you tried. Which you won't. Or else *I'll* be forced to arm-wrestle you."

A major crush? Stephanie thought. *Isn't it more than that? Doesn't Luke like me, too?* She remembered the way Luke had kissed her the day before.

Yes. Definitely!

"I told Tiffany and Stephanie that being a camp counselor means being ready for anything!" Heather announced to the crowd. "I'm not sure if they believed me. So I thought of the strangest task I could."

Stephanie was standing on the stage of the lodge next to Tiffany. She felt incredibly silly. Not only were all the Sail-Away campers standing and waiting, but the guys from Clearwater were there, too. The lodge was filled to capacity. All the tables had been moved out so that there was room for people to stand.

Stephanie spotted Luke standing in the back and smiled at him. She couldn't wait to get the tiebreaker over with—and start the dance.

Outside, lights were strung along the lodge porch, where a stereo was set up. There would be dancing on the main lawn, and snacks and punch, too. The camp photographer was roaming around with her camera. She had already taken one snapshot of Stephanie and Tiffany onstage.

"As you all know, we're about to have a party," Heather said. A loud cheer went up from the crowd. "And wouldn't the party get off to a great start if Stephanie and Tiffany delivered punch to everyone?" Heather pulled a sheet off the table behind her. Punch bowls with cups were placed on it.

"Brilliant idea!" Rene called up to Heather.

"Each girl will serve and deliver as many cups of punch as she can within a two-minute time period," Heather said.

"I love it!" Darah cried.

Stephanie glanced over at Tiffany to see if she liked the idea as much as her friends did. She was smiling triumphantly. That was when Stephanie noticed a few large purple stains on Tiffany's shirt.

"Wait a second," Stephanie said. "Have you been practicing ahead of time?"

"Me?" Tiffany put a hand to her throat.

"No, the *other* person with giant punch stains on her white T-shirt!" Stephanie said.

Heather stared at her, too. "Tiffany? How do you explain that?"

"This T-shirt *came* this way," Tiffany said. "It's, um, designer."

"Who's the designer?" Stephanie asked. "Cheaters, Inc.?"

"No! I did not cheat," Tiffany said. "Okay, if you want to know the truth, I was thirsty and I went into the kitchen and stole a cup of punch. But the cup was defective and it, like, came apart. Punch everywhere."

Stephanie's eyes narrowed. That sounded a little too convenient to her.

"Come on!" someone in the crowd yelled.

"Hurry up!"

"We're thirsty!"

"Okay, okay. I'm going to assume you didn't discover my plan ahead of time and practice," Heather told Tiffany. "But if I find out any differently, you'll have to answer to Mr. McCready."

"Yes, er, ma'am," Tiffany said in a frightened tone. She quickly took the left side of the table. Stephanie took the right.

"Nobody take a drink until the two minutes are up and I count the number of full cups!" Heather ordered the crowd. "Ready, girls? And . . . go!"

Stephanie first ladled several cups of punch. She knew it would be faster that way. She grabbed six and delivered them to people; then another six; then another six. She was working so fast, she didn't even notice who she was handing the cups to! She kept her head down and moved quickly.

When she ladled more cups of punch, she glanced over at Tiffany's side of the room. Only a few people were holding cups of punch, but Tiffany had several full cups sitting on the table, ready to go.

I've got to beat her! Stephanie thought with a determined push through the crowd. *I can't let the Flamingoes win this battle.*

"One minute to go!" Heather called out. "One minute!"

Stephanie lifted six more cups of punch. She was about to head to the middle of the room, when she saw people moving out of the corner of her eye. Better stay away from there, she thought. She made a quick move in the other direction.

"Agh! Look out!" Tiffany shrieked.

Stephanie looked over and saw Tiffany falling to the ground in a shower of purple punch! "Why did you *do* that?" Tiffany cried.

"Do what?" Darah said.

"You ran into me," Tiffany said.

"I wasn't trying to," Darah said. "I was trying to trip—never mind!" She hauled Tiffany to her feet. "Get moving!"

Tiffany just stood there, punch dripping out of her hair. "I'm not moving another inch."

Heather blew her whistle. "Time's up, girls! I was going to do a cup count, but I don't think it's necessary. It looks like Stephanie's going to be our winner. Congratulations, Stephanie! You did a great job."

"But this wasn't a fair competition," Rene complained.

"I can't believe *you're* going to talk about fair," Stephanie said as she walked over to her. "After you had Jenny fix the second day of the contest!"

Rene glared at Stephanie and then walked away from her. "Stephanie had more people standing on her side, so they were easier to get to! And then she got in Tiffany's way—"

"*Darah* got in my way, Rene," Tiffany cried. "And it was totally fair! Stephanie won, that's all. She'd make a better CIT, anyway."

"But what a stupid way to end such an intense competition," Rene said. "I mean—"

"It wasn't stupid!" Tiffany insisted. "I just lost, that's all."

"But after everything I did—" Jenny began.

"I didn't even want the job—you guys made me go for it," Tiffany cried. "So leave me alone! I'm going to change!" She ran out of the lodge.

Stephanie's friends surrounded her in a group hug. "See? This is going to be a fantastic summer after all!" Allie squeezed Stephanie tightly.

Stephanie released her friends and headed for the back of the lodge to find Luke. She didn't see him anywhere in the crowd that was quickly dispersing. She went outside and gazed around the porch.

"Stephanie? Are you looking for Luke?"

"Um . . . yeah." Stephanie paused as she walked past Max. He was standing at the far edge of the porch by himself.

"I haven't seen him for a while," Max said.

"That's okay, I'll find him on my own." Stephanie didn't want to talk to Max about Luke again. She felt disloyal for having listened to him bad-mouth Luke even once.

"Wait—hold up, Stephanie." Max hurried after her. "I know you think I just don't like Luke or something because we're so competitive. But that's not it."

"It isn't?" Stephanie asked.

Max shook his head. "No. See, there's more to that story I started to tell you the other day."

Stephanie folded her arms across her chest and faced Max. "What story?"

"I was about to tell you, when Luke came up. Someone vandalized the boathouse last summer," Max said.

"So?" Stephanie asked.

"So all the boats got cut loose and drifted off. Some of them were badly damaged," Max went on. "The boathouse was covered with spray paint. And Luke did it!"

"How do you know?" Stephanie asked.

"First, he wasn't at our camp meeting that night. Second, he works at the camp bike shop, where all the paint is. And third, someone found his keys down there when they discovered the damage. Face it, Stephanie—Luke isn't the nice guy you think he is!"

Stephanie's heart sank. She'd tried not to listen to all the bad things people told her about Luke. She liked him so much.

But all the rumors swirling around Luke were beginning to make her wonder. What if they were actually true?

What if Luke was nothing but trouble?

CHAPTER
15

♦ ◄ ▸ ♦

There's no real proof that Luke did anything, Stephanie thought. *There's got to be another explanation for the vandalism.*

"Luke could have dropped his keys anytime," she said to Max. "Maybe he missed the meeting because his parents were in town—"

"They weren't," Max said. "Look, Stephanie, everyone knew it was Luke. Why do you think he's not a junior counselor this summer, when he was a CIT last year?" he asked.

"Maybe he didn't want to be," Stephanie said. "Anyway, if he was the one who vandalized the boathouse, why didn't they kick him out? Why did they let him come back this summer?"

"Because there wasn't any hard proof," Max said. "But—"

"Maybe there wasn't any proof because Luke didn't do it," Stephanie said angrily. "Luke would never damage sailboats, or the boathouse—or anything! He lives for being on the water, boating, swimming, waterskiing—"

"Sure, he's *good* at all that stuff," Max said. "But, Stephanie, you don't know him like I do."

Stephanie couldn't believe Max was standing there accusing Luke when Luke wasn't around to defend himself. "I know Luke," she told Max. "And one thing I know is that he's not as dangerous as you and everyone else seem to think. He likes to take risks, sure—maybe he takes too many—but he's not a bad person."

"So you're right about him—and everyone else is wrong?" Max scoffed.

"I don't know why you have this huge grudge against Luke," Stephanie said. "But it's your problem—not mine. Luke has been nothing but nice to me. Now, if you don't mind, I want to start celebrating." She marched off toward the refreshment table. She didn't want to listen to Max for another minute.

* * *

Darcy came up while Stephanie was ladling punch at the punch bowl. "Hi, Darce. Want some?" she asked.

"Sure. Why not," Darcy said glumly. "Did you find Luke?"

"Not yet." Stephanie ladled two cups of the purple fruit punch and handed one to Darcy. "I can't believe I'm going to drink this stuff. I can't believe there's any *left* after Tiffany spilled it all."

She glanced at her friend's face. Darcy didn't seem to be having a very good time. "Is everything okay? How are things going with Keith?" she asked.

"Horrible," Darcy said. She sipped from her cup of punch.

"Why?" Stephanie asked.

"Take a look over there." Darcy gestured with her cup.

Stephanie saw Keith and Rene dancing together. "Oh, no," she groaned. "How did that happen?"

Darcy shrugged. "You know Rene. As soon as she finds out you like someone, she has to like him, too. They've been hanging out together for the past fifteen minutes. It's *torture* watching them."

"So look away." Stephanie pulled Darcy's arm and forced her to turn in the opposite direction.

"I still know they're there." Darcy crumpled her paper cup and threw it into the trash can.

All of a sudden a pair of hands covered Stephanie's eyes. Stephanie squealed. "Ack! Who is it? Darcy, tell me who it is."

"I'm not telling," Darcy said.

Stephanie struggled to pry the person's fingers off her face.

"Ow! You're going to break my finger!" a familiar voice cried.

"Luke!" Stephanie giggled. She was so excited to see Luke again. Never mind what Max said. She loved being around Luke. "You might as well let go—I know it's you."

"Okay, okay—it's me." Luke dropped his hands and squeezed Stephanie around the waist.

"Where have you been?" Stephanie asked as she turned to face him. "I was looking all over for you."

"I was busy. Looking all over for these." Luke pulled a bouquet of small orange and blue wildflowers from his back pocket. He had tied them together with brown twine. "When I saw you were going to win, I slipped outside to pick them for you. Congratulations!" He handed the bouquet to Stephanie.

She held the fresh flowers up to her nose and took a deep breath. "They smell wonderful— they're beautiful. Thanks!" She gave Luke a hug.

He held on and didn't let her go for a long while. "So, you want to dance?"

"Sure," Stephanie said softly into his ear. Then she remembered Darcy. She pulled away from Luke and looked for her friend. Darcy had already walked over to find Allie and Kayla. The three of them were heading out onto the lawn to dance.

"What are you waiting for?" Luke asked as he took Stephanie's hand.

"Nothing!" Stephanie grinned at him. She placed the bouquet carefully on a rock next to the table and took one flower out of the bouquet to stick in her hair. "I'll come back for the rest later," she told Luke. "Let's dance!"

She and Luke rushed over to dance next to Darcy and the others. *This is so great,* Stephanie thought. *All my best friends, a fabulous new boyfriend—and a new CIT job, too! This summer's turning out to be perfect after all.*

Luke tried to spin Stephanie around, and they

both cracked up laughing when she nearly fell down. When the song ended, Luke and Stephanie smiled at each other as they waited for the next one. Darcy started forming a conga line to dance around the edge of the lawn.

Stephanie joined the line, Luke right behind her, his hands on her waist.

Then, abruptly, the music stopped, mid-song.

"Hey!" Anna cried.

"Music, please!" Darcy called to the lodge steps, where the CD player and speakers were set up.

Stephanie looked up and saw a few counselors talking with Mr. McCready. "What happened?" she asked Luke.

"I don't know. Power outage?" he guessed.

Mr. McCready grabbed a microphone that was plugged into the stereo system. "Attention, please, everyone. May I have your attention?"

The crowd grew silent. "What's going on?" someone shouted.

"We hate to stop the party. We really do. But Mr. Davis has a very important announcement," Mr. McCready said. "Something's happened over at Clearwater."

Stephanie turned to Luke, her eyes wide. "What do you think—"

"Shh." Luke put his hand on Stephanie's elbow. "I have to hear this!"

"Good evening, everyone. I'm afraid I have some bad news," Mr. Davis began. "The main lodge over at Clearwater was seriously vandalized tonight."

Stephanie gasped. She felt Luke tighten his grip on her arm.

"Somebody broke in while we were all over here," Mr. Davis explained. "I went back to get some supplies we needed and discovered the damage. There are broken chairs, pots and pans strewn all over the kitchen—and paint has been sprayed all over the walls. It's a complete mess. Some of the damage is going to be very difficult—and expensive—to repair."

Stephanie glanced around the lawn. Everyone in the crowd was very concerned. People were whispering to each other or staring up at Mr. Davis. Stephanie hated the idea of someone's sneaking into either camp to damage property or steal things.

"Is anything missing? Was it a robbery?" one of the male counselors called out.

"We're not sure yet," Mr. Davis said. "So far it looks to me like an act of vandalism, plain and simple. And I don't know who's responsible. But whoever it is—whether the person is a camper or not—he or she will be punished. Camp Clearwater will not tolerate this kind of behavior!"

"And neither will Camp Sail-Away," Mr. McCready added quickly.

"If anyone knows anything, or hears anything—please don't hesitate. Come see me immediately," Mr. Davis said. "Because nobody here wants the person or persons responsible for this to get away with it—not this year."

Not this year! Stephanie felt a flutter of fear in her stomach. Mr. Davis was referring to what had happened the year before. He was talking about the boathouse vandalism. Was Luke responsible back then?

What if he's responsible now? Stephanie gazed at Luke's profile. He was biting his thumbnail and looking slightly nervous.

Why would he be nervous? Stephanie wondered. *Because people might suspect him after what happened the year before? Or because he did it again this year?*

She thought about how Luke had vanished from the party for a while. He'd said it was to pick flowers for her. What if he ran back to Clearwater instead?

Don't be ridiculous, Stephanie told herself as Luke turned to her with an awkward smile. *It can't be Luke.*

Can it?

CHAPTER
16

♦ ◄ ♦ ♦

"Sorry, guys—the party's over." Mr. McCready stepped to the railing as Mr. Davis left to return to the boys' camp.

Darcy groaned.

"We were just starting to have fun," Allie complained.

Stephanie looked at Luke and shrugged. "Well, so much for one last song."

Luke smiled. "They don't really get the concept of having a party, do they?" He glanced at his watch. "It's only nine o'clock."

"I want everyone—boys and girls—back in their cabins in half an hour," Mr. McCready said.

"You can do what you like until then—within reason, of course!"

"I want to see the Clearwater lodge," Darcy said. "You guys want to come along?"

"Will we have time?" Allie asked.

"If we run," Darcy said. "Come on!"

"Luke?" Stephanie asked. "Do you want to check it out?"

"Sure. If they'll let us in," Luke said.

"What do you mean?" Stephanie asked.

"They might be collecting evidence or something." Luke hustled down the path beside Stephanie.

"You make it sound so serious," Allie told him.

"I'm pretty sure that's how the camp directors are looking at it," Luke said.

"I think everyone else has the same idea we do," Stephanie commented as campers streamed down the path toward Clearwater. Mostly it was boys heading home to their cabins, but some other girls were going along, too. It was getting so crowded that it was hard to move quickly.

"Come on, you guys—follow me. I know a shortcut," Luke said.

Stephanie and her friends followed him as he branched off into the woods. *Luke knows a short-*

cut, Stephanie thought. *That means he can get back and forth between camps faster than other people can. Which means he could have been involved in the vandalism.*

Stop it, she chided herself. *You don't know anything for sure yet. Until you do, you have to trust Luke!*

"Good thing there's a full moon tonight," Kayla said as she ran behind Stephanie. "Otherwise I'd be flat on my face by now!"

"No kidding," Allie said. "Just how short is this shortcut?"

"It actually isn't that much faster," Luke told her. "But the fact we're the only ones on this path helps!"

They arrived at Clearwater about five minutes later. "We should have come by canoe," Darcy said as she wiped a few drops of sweat off her brow.

"That would have been fun," Kayla said. "Canoeing by moonlight sounds romantic." She winked at Stephanie. "But probably not with all of us along for the ride."

They headed for the lodge. All of the doors were wide open. Columns of campers filed in and out of the building as if they were on official tours.

"How bad is it?" Luke asked a boy as they climbed the steps.

"The place is trashed," he said. "Whoever did it must have had help."

Stephanie walked into the lodge and stopped short. "Wow," she said. The first things she noticed were all the upturned tables and chairs. A few chair legs were scattered on the floor. Stephanie started to step into the lodge, but a counselor inside reached out to stop her.

"Sorry," he said. "Too many visitors for one night. We need to start cleaning up."

"Oh. Well, can we help?" Stephanie offered.

"No, but thanks," he said. "Do you guys mind standing out on the porch? And remember, lights-out is at nine-thirty."

"We remember," Darcy told him. "We just wanted to see what it looked like."

"It's worse than I thought," Stephanie said.

Green neon paint covered the walls in swirls. There were painted goofy stick figures with the names of counselors and Mr. Davis underneath.

Luke laughed. "This is unreal!"

Stephanie glanced at him. She didn't see what was funny about it. "Do you think this is a joke or something?" she snapped.

"Sorry! But I can't help thinking maybe it *was* a practical joke," Luke said.

"Even if it was, it's not funny," Stephanie said. "What if this happened to your cabin? To my cabin? I'd hate it."

"True," Luke said. "But you can't take it too seriously. I mean, no one was hurt. And all it really boils down to is cleaning off paint and repairing some broken chairs. I mean, that *does* kind of look like Mr. Davis," Luke whispered in her ear as he pointed to the goofy drawing. "Doesn't it? Especially the curly hair."

Stephanie laughed and shook her head. "No, it doesn't."

"We'd better run," Kayla said. She pointed to the clock by the kitchen doors. "At least that isn't broken."

"It'd be nice if it was," Luke said. "Then we could use it as an excuse for being late the rest of the summer!"

Allie smiled at him. "I like the way you think." She pulled Stephanie aside and spoke in a softer voice. "We'll wait by the trail for you, so you don't walk back alone. But hurry up and say good night," Allie said.

"Okay—I'll be there in a couple of minutes," Stephanie said.

She and Luke stood just outside the doorway while the clean-up crew got to work on the lodge. The moon was shining directly above them, and the evening had finally turned cool.

"Tomorrow is Parents' Day for the younger kids," Luke told her. "No activities from one o'clock to three. Meet me at the Clearwater flag-pole—I'll get us a picnic lunch, and we can go for a hike together."

"I'll be there," Stephanie assured him.

Just then she spotted something shiny on the bottom of Luke's T-shirt. She stared at the green spot. *It can't be*, she thought. *It must be something else.*

She glanced through the window of the lodge at the paint-smeared walls. Then she checked Luke's shirt.

There was no doubt about it. The spot was green neon paint. Exactly the same shade of paint the vandal had used!

CHAPTER
17

♦ ◂ ▪ ♦

"Luke?" Stephanie knocked on the wooden door of Luke's cabin Sunday at noon. "Hello? Is anyone home? Luke?"

Stephanie had waited by the Clearwater flagpole for ten minutes. Just when she was about to go look for Luke, his counselor Charlie came by.

"Luke told me to tell you he'd been delayed," Charlie said. He checked his watch. "But he should be back to his cabin by now."

Stephanie had decided to check Luke's cabin. Now she knocked on his door again.

There was no answer. She slowly pushed the door open. "Hello?"

Nobody was inside the cabin. Stephanie decided to go in and wait. She'd brought a small card she'd made to apologize for grilling Luke about the green paint on his shirt the night before. He'd explained that the paint came from the bike shop, where he worked.

Of course, Stephanie thought now. *That made sense. As if Luke would have anything to do with vandalism.*

Stephanie gazed around the cabin, trying to pick out Luke's bunk. The interior looked pretty much like her cabin—or, at least, the cabin she had now. On Monday, Mr. McCready was going to hold a drawing and assign CITs to cabins for the rest of the summer.

I can't wait, Stephanie thought as she wandered over to a bunk bed and sat down to wait for Luke. *No more Rene!*

As soon as she sat down, Stephanie realized she was sitting directly across from what must be Luke's bunk. A poster of his favorite band was tacked to the wall. The book he had mentioned he was reading lay on his pillow, next to a bedside lamp made out of a water-skiing trophy with Luke's name on it.

The sun streamed through the window.

Something under Luke's bed glinted and caught Stephanie's eye. She strained to focus. *Were those aerosol cans?* she wondered, leaning forward. *Was that spray paint?*

I'm not trying to snoop, she told herself as she stood up and crouched beside Luke's bunk. *I'm just curious, that's all.* She reached underneath and pulled out one of the cans.

It was bright-green neon spray paint—and the can was completely empty. Stephanie grabbed another can. It was empty, too. Stuck to the bottom of it was a sheet of notebook paper. Stephanie stared at the writing on it.

"This is a list," she murmured. "A list of all the damage the vandals did last night!"

Suddenly the cabin door creaked and swung open. "Stephanie? What are you doing down there?"

Stephanie jumped up and hit her head on the top bunk bed.

"Oh, no!" Luke hurried over toward her. "Are you okay?"

"Yes. No!" Tears filled Stephanie's eyes. She held the list in one hand and an empty paint can in the other.

"Did you hurt yourself?" Luke asked. He

reached out to touch Stephanie's head. "I think I feel a lump—"

"Stop it!" Stephanie cried as she backed away from him.

"Sorry. I didn't know it hurt that much," Luke said.

"It doesn't," Stephanie said. "But this does." She shoved the paint can toward him. "I found this under your bed. You told me you had had nothing to do with the vandalism at the lodge!"

Luke took the can from her and stared at it. "I didn't."

"Then, how come I found this stuff here? Even this list—is that your handwriting?" Stephanie asked. She brushed a tear off her cheek as Luke studied the piece of paper.

"No! This looks like my handwriting," Luke said, "but it isn't. I didn't write this!"

Stephanie shook her head. "I don't believe you!"

"Stephanie, please—you've got to," Luke begged. He put his hand on her arm as Stephanie tried to leave the cabin.

"No, I don't believe you. And I can't—not anymore!" She pushed past Luke. The tears in her eyes nearly blinded her as she stumbled out of the cabin.

Everyone tried to warn me about Luke, Stephanie thought. *I wouldn't listen. But they were right—Luke is completely the wrong guy for me.*

I wish I'd never met him!

WIN A $500 SHOPPING SPREE AT THE WARNER BROTHERS STUDIO STORE!

1 Grand Prize: A $500 shopping spree at the Warner Brothers Studio Store

----

Complete entry form and send to: Pocket Books/ "Full House Club Stephanie Sweepstakes"
1230 Avenue of the Americas, 13th Floor, NY, NY 10020

NAME _____ **BIRTHDATE** ___ /___ /___

ADDRESS _____

CITY _____ **STATE** _____ **ZIP** _____

PHONE (_____) _____

PARENT OR LEGAL GUARDIAN'S SIGNATURE *(required for entrants under 18 years of age at date of entry.)*

_____

   See back for official rules.

Pocket Books/ "Full House Club Stephanie Sweepstakes"
Sponsors Official Rules:

No Purchase Necessary.

Enter by mailing this completed Official Entry Form (no copies allowed) or by mailing a 3" x 5" card with your name and address, daytime telephone number and birthdate to the Pocket Books/ "Full House Club Stephanie Sweepstakes", 1230 Avenue of the Americas, 13th Floor, NY, NY 10020. Entry forms are available in the back of Full House Club Stephanie #10: Truth or Dare (6/00), #11: Summertime Secrets (7/00) and #12: The Real Thing (8/00), on in-store book displays and on the web site SimonSaysKids.com. Sweepstakes begins 6/1/00. Entries must be postmarked by 8/31/00 and received by 9/15/00. Sponsors are not responsible for lost, late, damaged, postage-due, stolen, illegible, mutilated, incomplete, or misdirected or not delivered entries and mail or for typographical errors in the entry form or rules or for telecommunications system or computer software or hardware errors or data loss. Entries are void if they are in whole or in part illegible, incomplete or damaged. Enter as often as you wish, but each entry must be mailed separately. Winner will be selected at random from all eligible entries received in a drawing to be held on or about 9/25/00. The Winner will be notified by phone.

Prizes: One Prize: A $500 shopping spree at the Warner Brothers Studio Store. (retail value: $500).

The sweepstakes is open to legal residents of the U.S. (excluding Puerto Rico) and Canada (excluding Quebec) ages 6-10 as of 8/31/00. Proof of age is required to claim prize. Prize will be awarded to the winner's parent or legal guardian. Void wherever prohibited or restricted by law. All federal, state and local laws apply. Simon & Schuster, Inc., Parachute Publishing, Warner Bros. and their respective officers, directors, shareholders, employees, suppliers, parent companies, subsidiaries, affiliates, agencies, sponsors, participating retailers, and persons connected with the use, marketing or conduct of this sweepstakes are not eligible. Family members living in the same household as any of the individuals referred to in the preceding sentence are not eligible.

Prize is not transferable and may not be substituted except by sponsors, in the event of prize unavailability, in which case a prize of equal or greater value will be awarded. The odds of winning the prize depend upon the number of eligible entries received.

If the winner is a Canadian resident, then he/she must correctly answer a skill-based question administered by mail.

All expenses on receipt and use of prize including federal, state and local taxes are the sole responsibility of the winner. Winner's parents or legal guardians may be required to execute and return an Affidavit of Eligibility and Publicity Release and all other legal documents which the sweepstakes sponsors may require (including a W-9 tax form) within 15 days of attempted notification or an alternate winner may be selected.

Winner or winner's parents or legal guardians on winner's behalf agree to allow use of winner's name, photograph, likeness, and entry for any advertising, promotion and publicity purposes without further compensation to or permission from the entrant, except where prohibited by law.

Winner and winner's parents or legal guardians agree that Simon & Schuster, Inc., Parachute Publishing and Warner Bros. and their respective officers, directors, shareholders, employees, suppliers, parent companies, subsidiaries, affiliates, agencies, sponsors, participating retailers, and persons connected with the use, marketing or conduct of this sweepstakes, shall have no responsibility or liability for injuries, losses or damages of any kind in connection with the collection, acceptance or use of the prize awarded herein, or from participation in this promotion.

By participating in this sweepstakes, entrants agree to be bound by these rules and the decisions of the judges and sweepstakes sponsors, which are final in all matters relating to the sweepstakes. Failure to comply with the Official Rules may result in a disqualification of your entry and prohibition of any further participation in this sweepstakes.

The first name of the winner will be posted at SimonSaysKids.com or the first name of the winner may be obtained by sending a stamped, self-addressed envelope after 9/31/00 to Prize Winners, Pocket Books "Full House Club Stephanie Sweepstakes," 1230 Avenue of the Americas, 13th Floor, NY, NY 10020.

*Don't miss out on any of
Stephaine and Michelle's
exciting adventures!*

FULL HOUSE™

SISTERS

*When sisters get together...
expect the unexpected!*

A MINSTREL® BOOK

Published by Pocket Books

2012-03